PRAISE FOR THE FIERY TALES

"Evocative, erotic. . . [A] sensual treat!"
— **Sylvia Day,**
#1 *New York Times* bestselling author

"Hot enough to warm the coldest winter night."
— **Publishers Weekly**

"Sophisticated and deeply romantic."
—**Elizabeth Hoyt,**
New York Times bestselling author

"Sure to delight!"
— **Jennifer Ashley,**
New York Times bestselling author

"The most luscious, sexy take on classic fairy tales
I've ever read!"
—**Cheryl Holt,**
New York Times bestselling author

"Sets the classic fairy tale(s) ablaze!"
—**Anna Campbell,**
bestselling, award-winning author

The Marquis's New Clothes

A Fiery Tale

LILA DIPASQUA

DiPasqua

Excerpt from *The Lovely Duckling*, in *The Princess in His Bed* anthology by Lila DiPasqua copyright © Lila DiPasqua
Cover Design: Carrie Divine/Seductive Designs

Photography of couple: © Period Images;

Interior Design by Woven Red Author Services, www.WovenRed.ca

PRINTING HISTORY
First Edition: From *The Princess in His Bed*, Berkley Sensation/Penguin Group (USA) Inc.—November 2010
Second Edition: Lila DiPasqua—October 2016

ISBN: 978-0-9951655-3-3 (trade pbk)
ISBN: 978-0-9951655-2-6 (e-book)

To the man who inspired the hero in this story—my very own wonderful husband, who, like Adam de Vey, happens to be an engineer.

Thank you for your scientific input in The Marquis's New Clothes. And for your unwavering support and belief in me.

I love you, Carm.

CHAPTER ONE

Palace of Versailles, 1683

"My life is over!" Louise d'Arcy exclaimed the moment after she'd yanked Aimee inside her elegant private apartments and slammed the door shut.

Aimee de Miran sighed. She'd just arrived at Versailles. Her sojourn at the palace was only ten minutes long and already she was rethinking her plan to attend court and visit with her cousin.

Dear Louise was always in the midst of chaos. It seemed now was no different.

Parched from the long carriage ride, Aimee walked over to the pitcher of water and orange slices on the ebony side table and promptly filled two crystal goblets. "Louise, darling, I'm certain your life isn't over." She held a goblet out to her cousin. "Now why don't you tell me what's wrong."

"What's wrong? Renault is what's wrong. He's cast me aside!" Wringing her hands, Louise began to pace, completely oblivious to Aimee's extended arm and the goblet of fresh water being offered.

Aimee availed herself of the refreshment instead and set the goblet down.

A lovers' spat. Nothing new.

"I see." That would be all she'd need to say for the next hour while Louise ranted. When she was done, her cousin would collapse in a chair, quite theatrically, and weep for at least twenty more minutes.

Aimee had been through this before. Many times. Louise was always having spats with her longtime lover, Renault de Sard.

Louise stopped dead in her tracks. "No, you don't see. You've no idea what has occurred. Everything is a mess. And it's over this time! Truly over!" Her hazel eyes filled with tears. "He'll not have anything more to do with me. He's said so!" She dropped her face into her palms and sobbed.

Aimee approached and put a consoling arm around her cousin. Of similar age, they'd always been close. She did adore Louise, despite her histrionics. "Louise, it will work out. You'll see. He always comes back."

"Not this time," she said without lifting her head, the words muffled by her hands.

"You say that every time."

Her cousin's head shot up. "This time it's true!"

"You say *that* every time, too."

Louise let out a sharp breath. "Aimee, he favors another! I have been replaced. He's with Diane de Millon. I'm no longer his mistress at all! I tell you, he is a horrible, *horrible* cad! He purposely misled me."

"Oh? Misled you how?"

"I was positively thrilled when he asked me to accompany him to the palace for his regular official visit with the King. He'd been so cold and distant lately that I didn't think he'd permit me to attend this time. In truth, his plan was to bring me here to end our affair. He thought I wouldn't pitch a fit at the palace. And do you know what I did?'

"You pitched a fit at the palace."

"No. Well . . . yes." Louise waved her hand dismissively. "But that was in private. And that's not what I'm talking about." Her cousin began to pace and wring her hands again. "I did something. Something terrible. Something I regret."

Trepidation was beginning to mount in Aimee. Louise always had a flare for the dramatic, but . . . Aimee couldn't shake the disquieting feeling tightening in her stomach. There was a certain look in Louise's eyes that made her a little anxious.

"What did you do?"

Her cousin smoothed her hands down her gown. A habit. Something Louise always did when she was nervous. Or uneasy. Or terribly guilty.

"Well, you see . . ." Louise began and smoothed her hands down her gown again. "You must understand, I was quite angry with Renault at the time, and very hurt by his cutting coldness toward me. So I . . ."

Aimee braced herself. Having no idea what she was about to hear, her instincts told her it was going to be bad. Quite bad. "You *what*?"

"I took something of his."

"Took?"

"All right, I *stole*. There, I said it. Is that better? I *stole* something he holds dear."

Good Lord. This was a new low, even for Louise. "What on earth did you steal?"

Louis threw up her hands. "The man has never given me *anything*, Aimee. In all these years, no lover's trinket. No jewelry at all! I felt he owed me at least that much."

Aimee struggled with her patience. "Louise . . . What. Did. You. Take?"

"His jeweled ring. One of the ones given to him by the King."

"Oh, Louise, you didn't."

"I did!" Louise flopped down onto the nearby chair, dropped her face into her palms again, and wept audibly.

Aimee shook her head, dismayed. Of all the predicaments Louise had landed herself in, this one was by far the most shocking. "Didn't it occur to you that Renault is the King's Lieutenant General of *Police*? A man who is overzealous when it comes to the duties of his post and would arrest his own mother for the most minor infraction?"

Louise looked up. "Well, not at the time, but it certainly has over the last few hours . . ." She choked on a sob. "What am I going to do? My life is over! He'll throw me in one of those horrible cells without batting an eye. If he's angry enough, he could have orders drawn up against me, and I'll be held without trial—for who knows how long."

Aimee took in a fortifying breath and let it out slowly. She walked over to her distressed kin and placed a hand on her shoulder. "Everything is going to be fine. We can remedy this problem. This really isn't as great a dilemma as you think it is."

Her cousin swiped away the tears on her cheek. "Oh, but it is."

"No it isn't. You will return the ring with a sincere apology–"

"I can't."

"You're right. The man is so rigid and uncompromising, he won't understand," Aimee said as an idea occurred to her. "I have it. You'll sneak into his rooms and put the ring back, without him being the wiser."

"I can't do that either."

Aimee frowned. "What do you mean, you can't?"

"I lost the ring."

"You *what?*"

Louise rose from the chair. "Well, it's not entirely lost. I know where it is. Sort of."

"Where in the name of God is it—*sort of?*"

"I had it with me when I was in the Hall of Mirrors yesterday. It was very crowded, as usual. I was bumped from behind, and it fell out of my hand and into the pocket of one of the courtiers."

"Do you know who?"

"I do. The Marquis de Nattes."

Aimee's heart missed a beat. "Adam de Vey, Marquis de Nattes?" she questioned, hoping she'd heard wrong.

"Yes. Exactly." Her cousin grasped Aimee's hands and squeezed them. "Aimee, I can't let Renault learn what I did. If the ring is found on the Marquis de Nattes's person, Renault would never believe he stole the ring. He has one of his own from the King. You must help me get the ring back before Renault discovers it missing. He'll not stop until he uncovers the thief. Me!"

This was only getting worse. She didn't like the direction this conversation was taking. "What exactly are you suggesting I do?"

For the first time since Aimee entered the room, her cousin smiled. "You know as well as I do the Marquis de Nattes would be receptive to any attention you would give him. Since Marc died, he looks at you 'that' way. You could easily get close enough to him to search his clothes."

Aimee's brows shot up. "Have you gone mad? You want me to encourage that libertine just so I can dip my hands in his pockets in search of your ring?"

"Precisely. And perhaps you can search his armoire in his private apartments, too. The man does have a rather extensive wardrobe . . ."

"No. Absolutely not." Adam de Vey was the worst sort of man. The very type she detested. He was no different than her late husband. Beautiful as sin. A master at seduction.

And completely faithless.

A man who believed women were interchangeable. Who cared nothing of what he did to a woman's heart. Only what he did with her body.

It was no wonder that the Marquis de Nattes and her late husband, Marc, Comte de Gremont, had been friends. They were of like mind and poor character. Since Marc's death on the dueling field three years ago—a duel over his favorite paramour at the time—Aimee thankfully had had nothing more to do with her late husband's licentious friends.

Louise's bottom lip began to tremble, her eyes welling with fresh tears. "Renault will show me no mercy. He cares nothing for me at all now. If—If you don't help me . . . then I will surely be arrested, Aimee. You won't let that happen, will you? You'll help me, won't you?"

The pitiful look on her cousin's face tugged at Aimee's heart fiercely. She wanted to help her, but . . . she'd noticed the lingering looks Adam had given her since Marc's death, too. The last thing she wanted to do was to make him believe she'd be receptive to him.

"Louise . . . There's got to be another way . . ."

"There isn't! Oh, please, Aimee. I haven't anyone else who can help . . . I know you don't care for Adam de Vey, but think of it this way: You can do something most women cannot. You can easily flirt with Adam, yet resist him, and in the end do what no female has done—rebuff him."

Now, that did have a certain appeal. Men like the Marquis de Nattes toyed with so many women, luring them with their polished manner, potent sensuality, their false affections. She would definitely love to play him. Lure him. She could flirt a little. Draw close enough to locate the ring and save Louise.

She was likely one of the few women in the realm who'd resist his allure.

After giving herself over to her husband—heart, body, and soul—leaving herself open to the humiliation and heartbreak she'd ultimately endured, Aimee knew she'd never fall into the arms of another rake like Marc again.

"All right," tumbled from her mouth.

Louise squeaked with joy and threw her arms around Aimee. "Thank you! I knew I could count on your help."

Aimee sighed. "I don't suppose you have any idea what he was wearing when you dropped the ring?"

"I do!" Louise was finally smiling again. "He was wearing a blue justacorps."

"Blue? That's it?"

"I know how much the man adores fine clothing, and I did hear he had a new wardrobe delivered two days ago, but really, how many blue justacorps could he have in all?"

True. But given the number of knee-length coats he owned, what were the chances he'd wear the same blue justacorps again anytime soon?

Just how mindful was he of such things?

"Between the two of us, we'll be able to locate the ring quickly and easily," Louise said confidently.

Aimee couldn't believe she'd become embroiled in this mad plan. Outfoxing a seasoned roué; locating and lifting a ring out from under the nose of a man who, by his very womanizing nature, was highly attuned to the opposite sex. Reading women was his forte. He knew how to detect signs of amorous interest and sexual desire. Her performance would have to be believable and flawless, despite her limited skills at being a coquette.

Success hinged on her ability to stay focused. The problem was, she hadn't been touched by a man in over three long, empty years. Though she'd never admit it to anyone, she yearned to have a man's arms around her. The press of his hard body against hers. His body inside her. Her marriage bed had been most satisfying. Too satisfying. There had been many nights she wished her late husband had never introduced her to the pleasures of sex. That his conjugal visits had been more typical of his peers—brief. Obligatory. For the purposes of procreation only.

Awakening her to physical delights had caused her nothing but suffering.

For many reasons.

But no matter how much she desired a lover, she *wouldn't* take a man like the Marquis de Nattes to satisfy her carnal cravings.

For Louise's sake, Aimee had to succeed. She couldn't fail. She *would* best Adam in this cat and mouse game they were about to play.

And she was going to use his libertine nature to her advantage.

*****

Adam de Vey, Marquis de Nattes, surveyed the various justacorps—fitted knee-length coats of various fabrics and colors. He'd had a second armoire placed in his private rooms to hold his recently arrived new clothes.

Doors to both armoires were open wide as he decided on his attire for the afternoon. The news of Aimee's arrival made his selection a little more important. Made his heart beat faster, and his blood course hotter just knowing she was close by.

Adam couldn't believe his luck. Just when he'd reached his breaking point. Just when he'd been racking his mind, trying to orchestrate an opportunity to spend time under the same roof with the dark-haired beauty, she fortuitously showed up at the palace. He'd no idea when he'd been summoned by the King for an official meeting that she'd be in attendance at Versailles as well.

It was a good sign. A great sign. Somehow the stars had aligned and he was getting what he'd been wishing for for years. Access to Aimee. She wouldn't be able to leave anytime soon either. The King took personal offense to brief visits at the palace.

Her stay would have to be no less than half a month. Plenty of time for him to do something he'd dreamed about far too often.

Bed her.

It was going to be a challenge—his very first when it came to seducing a woman.

Dressed in black breeches and a white linen shirt, he watched as his loyal servant pulled out yet another justacorps, this one gold-colored, and brought it to him.

Adam touched the silk sleeve. "Not this one, Laurent," he said. Too bold.

The man, ten years his senior, returned the gold overcoat to the armoire.

"Really, Adam, I don't understand your interest in all these clothes." Reclining in a plush chair, his fingers laced behind his head, his friend Robert, Comte de Senville, smiled.

"I like the finer things in life. Fine clothes. A fine château. Fine women." Aimee de Miran was by far the finest he'd ever laid eyes on.

"How is this, my lord?" Laurent held before him a red justacorps.

Also bold. "I don't think so."

He was looking for something more understated. A quiet elegance. Just like Aimee.

"All this trouble for a tumble. Don't think I don't know you're planning on seducing Aimee de Miran. And it's about time, I say." Chuckling, Robert crossed his arms over his chest and shook his head. "Six years . . . *Dieu!*"

Adam placed his hands on his hips, cursing the night he'd gotten drunk last month and let it slip to Robert about his long-time fascination with their dead friend's wife.

Ignoring Robert's irksome remarks was easier than ignoring his own hardened cock—his body's natural reaction at the mere thought of the lovely Comtesse de Gremont.

From the moment he'd met her, during her betrothal to Marc, he'd been fiercely attracted to her. He'd spent a ridiculous amount of time famished for this woman.

Merde. He could make no sense of this incessant, unbreakable pull to her. His desire for her plagued him. Haunted him. The longer it went on, the more it tormented him.

The stronger it got.

So she was beautiful, elegant, graceful, and intelligent. There were others who shared those qualities. So Marc had boasted that his wife was passionate and sensual and highly receptive to his husbandly rights—a woman who saw her marriage bed as enjoyable rather than as a duty.

So what?

There were other women who enjoyed sex. He'd fucked scores of them.

Nothing he did got golden-eyed Aimee de Miran out of his head. Out of his system. Not time. Or women. He was tired of wanting her—and worse, comparing other women to her. It drove him to distraction.

Jésus-Christ. He couldn't recall the last time he'd bedded a woman when Aimee hadn't intruded into his mind, where he didn't fantasize it was her he was buried inside.

For the last six years, Adam had kept his distance from Marc's beautiful wife for two reasons. First and foremost, Aimee was in love with her husband, and he never poached where real feelings were involved. Second, Marc was a friend—one who was completely undeserving of his wife's affections. Marc knew full well he'd stirred her heart. He'd laughed about it and found it "adorable," and without discretion of any kind, bedded every woman who crossed his path.

"What about the blue, my lord?"

Adam scrutinized the blue-gray justacorps held out before him.

It was of the finest cloth, yet not boastful. And a fine cut, too. "Perfect."

"I think the lady will be most impressed, my lord." Laurent smiled as he handed him the matching vest—Laurent's usual statement whenever he sensed Adam had a new conquest in mind.

Adam slipped on his vest. "Do you now, Laurent."

"I think you overestimate your charm." Adam could hear the humor in Robert's tone.

He glanced at Robert. "I think you should leave the lady to me and concern yourself with the King, and whether or not he'll approve of our drawings and ideas." Adam slipped on the justacorps with Laurent's assistance.

A member of the Royal Academy of Sciences, Adam was recognized for his engineering expertise. Over the years, he'd worked on a number of projects for the Crown—particularly, the fortification of strongholds in case of attack. Now with the country at peace, at least for the time being, Louis had turned his attention to his prized palace.

Versailles.

Unhappy with the water pressure of his fountains, His Majesty had asked Adam to offer a solution to rectify the deficiency the original engineers had produced.

Robert stood and walked over to him, grinning. "It's far more fun watching Adam de Vey fail for the first time with a woman." He placed his hand on Adam's shoulder. "In all seriousness, the lady doesn't much care for either of us. Marc broke her heart. She sees us as being no different than her late husband."

That much he knew.

But Adam wasn't looking for her love. Or to replace Marc in her heart, if he was still there. He was looking for a few hours of shared carnal pleasure. He simply wanted to, no—had to—put an end to this inexplicable mental and physical torment. And there was only one way to kill the longing—and that was to have Aimee every which way he could to sate his lust for her.

Success hinged on his ability to stay focused. Patient. Unfortunately, just as Robert stated, she disliked him.

"I'll succeed," Adam said.

Robert lifted a dark brow. "You're that confident?"

"I am."

A slight smile lifted the corner of Robert's mouth. "Oh, I can't wait to see this. I predict she'll run the other way each time you draw near."

A realistic prediction.

For his sanity's sake, he had to succeed. He couldn't fail. He *would* best her in this cat and mouse game they were about to play. Beautiful, passionate Aimee hadn't had a lover since Marc's death. He'd left his wife at their country château while he'd carried on with his favorite mistress in the city, and hadn't been anywhere near her for months prior to his fatal duel. In short, she hadn't been touched in a very long time.

And she was ripe for the taking.

Adam was going to use her passionate nature to his advantage.

CHAPTER TWO

"Is that the blue justacorps he wore when you dropped the ring?" Aimee asked her cousin, her eyes fixed on Adam's tall sculpted form.

In the gardens of Versailles, scores of courtiers stood about, lords and ladies murmuring among themselves. The violinists that followed King Louis XIV around the gardens all day stood still, but continued to play, their music sweetening the warm summer air. The King had motioned everyone back, His Majesty wanting only Adam de Vey and Robert de Senville near. The three men stood at the Dragon Fountain in deep discussion, His Majesty listening intently to Adam's comments.

Unable to stop herself, she took in his strong, muscled body, his handsome profile. Few men were as tall as the King. Yet Adam stood well above His Majesty. As the King demanded of all men at court, Adam wore his periwig. Though away from court, the periwig was nowhere to be found. And she knew that underneath it, he had hair as dark as a raven's wig that matched his dark velvety eyes. Gorgeous, fathomless eyes that lured a woman in.

Despite the man's lascivious character, he was beautiful beyond belief.

Highly attractive men with disarming charm were the very bane of a woman's existence. A wicked promise always shone in their eyes. It drew women, despite their better judgment. Aimee understood the allure well. She'd been one of those women. She'd allowed herself to be drawn in by Marc in the same helpless, pathetic way. She should have limited her husband to her body. Yet she'd foolishly relinquished her heart as well.

Louise had her head tilted to one side studying Adam when Aimee finally dragged her gaze away from him.

"Well?" Aimee prompted.

"I'm not sure . . ." her cousin said. "It could be."

"Louise, that answer is no help at all."

"I'm sorry. It's difficult to remember!" Louise looked about. "Do you see Renault? Is he here? Is he with his mistress?"

"Stop looking for him," Aimee cautioned and added sotto voce, "Until we locate the ring, you're to keep your distance." Hopefully, Renault would keep his. For his years of loyal service, the man thankfully had two rings from the King. According to Louise, his finger was always adorned with one. Aimee was fairly confident he hadn't noticed his other was missing—*yet*.

Just then, the King began to walk, a signal for others to follow. He moved away from Adam, Robert, and the fountain, out toward the east side of the vast gardens.

Adam, who had been speaking to Robert, looked past his shoulder, his gaze meeting hers. A slight smile raised the corner of his sensuous mouth and he gave her a nod.

"Oh, my . . . Adam is looking this way." Louise pointed out the obvious.

"Yes, I know."

"Well, what should we do?"

Aimee returned his smile and nod. She thought something akin to surprise flashed in his eyes but it was so quick, she couldn't be certain. "If I'm going to do this, I might as well start now."

Feed into his conceit— that every woman is interested in him. Be bold. And if luck was on her side, locate the ring in the pocket of the very justacorps he was wearing. Out of mourning, she'd make him believe she was a lonely widow, looking for a lover. The fact that she really was a lonely widow who could truly use a lover should only make her performance easier. No?

As the crowd thinned down to a few stragglers, Aimee marched straight up to her late husband's notoriously rakish friends, Louise quickly on her heels.

Stopping before them, Aimee heard Robert saying, "She's not going to come over—" He choked back his words when he noticed her.

"Good day, Madame de Gremont." Robert quickly stepped forward with an instant smile and, taking her hand, pressed a kiss to her knuckle.

"Good day." Aimee returned Robert's greeting and his smile. Then turned to Adam as Robert moved to greet Louise.

Adam stepped into Robert's spot and took her hand. "Good day, Aimee." His familiarity momentarily unbalanced her. He'd never addressed her so informally. The way he'd said her name—so low and sensuously—caused a flutter in her belly. A ludicrous reaction that took her by surprise. A reaction that dismayed her. One she wasn't going to repeat.

Adam didn't kiss her hand immediately, as Robert had. Instead, he held her gaze, a half smile still gracing his lips. With the lightest stroke on the back of her hand, his thumb whispered across her skin. Tiny tingles sped up her arm and rippled to the tips of her breasts. Arresting her breath. Then he bent, his eyes still locked to hers, and pressed his warm mouth to her hand, causing her heart to quicken. And her thoughts to momentarily scatter. His lips lingered for a moment longer than was necessary before he stepped back and released her hand.

She blinked, stunned. He'd never, *ever*, greeted her like this before. Realizing her mouth had fallen agape, she clamped it shut. *Good God. There's no doubt about it; he is trying to seduce you.* And heaven help her, he was far too good at the game of seduction. He was pure sexual temptation. Even better at unraveling a woman than Marc had been. A mere touch had had the most unsettling effect. Worse, the look in his eyes told her he knew exactly what he'd done to her insides.

Aimee managed to force out a greeting, mentally cringing over how awkward she sounded.

Thankfully, Adam ignored the clumsiness of her response and moved to greet Louise. His greeting of her cousin was completely proper and entirely different from the one he'd just offered her.

Chastising herself for her physical responses to him, Aimee took a deep breath and returned her smile to her face. She had a job to do. And the sooner this was over, the better.

Focus . . .

"It is good to see you, gentlemen," she said, her voice thankfully belying her disquiet. "I wondered if you would be so kind as to be our escorts through the gardens?" She looked pointedly at Adam. "My cousin and I would be most appreciative." The crowd of courtiers was well ahead now.

His smile grew. "It would be my pleasure." He offered his arm.

He had an incredible smile. Quite perfect, actually.

Taking Adam's arm, she walked along, trying not to notice the muscle and sinew under her hand that was entirely too easy to detect, even through his clothing. Or how his strong hard body moved with such riveting masculine grace.

Her traitorous body began to warm.

With her cousin and Robert walking behind, Aimee tried to think of something to say. A topic of conversation, any distraction at all that would take her mind off the mounting heat rushing through her system.

"You look lovely, Aimee. Blue is most becoming on you," he said, his dark gaze dropping ever so briefly to her décolletage. Her nipples hardened.

Oh God. Much to her mortification, Aimee felt a blush coming on. She hadn't blushed in years.

You haven't had a man in years either. Compose yourself!

"Thank you. It's my favorite color," she lied. "I love to wear it. I love to see others wear it, too. Any shade, really. It draws my eyes to them immediately." Excellent recovery. Since he was trying to bed her, he'd definitely wear what pleased her.

And nothing would please her more than to locate the ring quickly.

"Really. I'll keep that in mind," he said. "I must admit, it was a pleasant surprise to see you approach," he continued. "I didn't think you cared much for me or Robert."

Perhaps she'd been too bold in approaching him. Perhaps she should have waited for him to approach her. The last thing she wanted was to raise his suspicions—that she was up to something.

"I'm sorry to hear that." Gravel crunched under her feet as they moved along the path. "I didn't realize I gave you that impression. It was not my intention, Monsieur de—"

"Adam," he interjected. "Simply Adam. No need for titles, Aimee. We've known each other a long time."

Mostly from afar—and by reputation. She'd heard more than one woman atwitter about gorgeous Adam de Vey and his carnal talents. Her husband's friends didn't visit the château. She only saw them when she was in the city, and since Marc's death, she'd tried to avoid them whenever possible.

"All right. Adam it is, then." She smiled, though her heart thudded in her chest. "You certainly had the attention of the King just now." *That's right. Make idle conversation and come up with a way to check those pockets.*

"Yes. His Majesty has summoned me for a meeting. He's displeased," he said, still smiling.

Her brows furrowed. "With you?"

"With his fountains. He wants me to fix them."

She glanced back at the Dragon Fountain that was now silent and no longer spraying water as it had moments ago. "You know how?"

"To fix them? Yes. It's going to be costly and require work, but it can be done."

She was intrigued. She thought he—like Marc—didn't know how to do anything other than indulge in vice.

"What's wrong with the fountains?" she asked, genuinely curious.

He lifted a brow. "You really wish to know?"

"Yes," she responded without hesitation.

This was novel for Adam. It was the first time she was actually talking to him, touching him. And for very first time in his life, he was going to discuss science with a stiff prick. In fact, she had him stiff as stone from the moment he caught her looking at him. There was no doubt about it; she'd reacted to his touch and the kiss on her hand.

And that delectable thought tightened his sac and raced his heart.

He didn't know why, but her interest in the fountains pleased him immensely. Most women wouldn't have cared to ask more questions, the subject too dull for their taste. He was as delighted about her curiosity as he was by her bold approach and request for an escort. Especially since he'd been sure he was going to have to corner her for any sort of conversation.

Celebrating in the turn of events, he silenced any questions he had regarding her uncharacteristic behavior.

"There are a number of fountains throughout the gardens," he explained. "There isn't enough water pressure to have them spout water at the same time and with the majestic height the King desires, so the fountains are turned on and off one at a time as the King approaches and leaves during his strolls around the gardens. But he wants them working all at the same time, in the same way."

"Really? I hadn't noticed until now . . . How will you fix them?"

"Since the water is presently being rerouted from the Seine—"

"All the way from Paris?" she injected, her eyes widened.

"Yes, all the way from Paris. The distance is significant, and the elevation of the land where the palace is located is high, both factors contributing to the problem. We are going to use a special machine, a pump, to draw the water."

"Will that work, your 'pump' machine?"

"It should. Robert and I have made a number of calculations. I've done up detailed drawings. We'll be showing them to the King later. I think he'll be pleased."

"And how is it you know so much about such things?"

Still she hadn't lost interest or become bored. Those beautiful golden-colored eyes were fixed on him the entire time, giving him her rapt attention.

He stopped walking and turned to face her, a smile tugging at the corners of his mouth. Yet another first. When all he'd ever done was fantasize about bedding her, he never would have guessed he'd derive such pleasure from a simple conversation with her.

Robert and Louise d'Arcy walked on past, involved in their own conversation.

"Science is a passion of mine," he said, without boasting about his reputation in the area or his achievements that had earned him the esteem of the King.

Mirth entered her eyes. She lifted her chin a notch. "Really? I thought women were a passion of yours."

One particular woman had become an obsession of his, truth be told.

Adam slipped his hand under her chin and brought it up a notch more, their lips so very close together. She drew in a sharp breath, surprised by his unexpected action. "You hardly know me, Aimee . . . so I will tell you, I am a man of many passions."

He saw something flash in her eyes before her gaze briefly dropped to his mouth. *An excellent sign.* His fever for her spiked. Her breathing had increased. Her skin was flushed. Drawing from his experience with women, he knew he was right about his golden-eyed beauty. A sexual encounter with Aimee would be nothing short of raw and intense. She *was* hungry. Naturally passionate. *She wants a lover.* It wouldn't take much to coax her into sex.

As he stared down at her upturned face, her perfect lush mouth, he wondered what she would do if he kissed her here and now. His instincts told him she'd succumb to it, to him, in a sweet surrender, unable to stop herself. The notion was delicious. As delicious as she was going to be in bed. His cock didn't just ache for her. Every fiber of his being ached for this one woman. Still holding her chin, Adam brushed his thumb across her soft bottom lip with a gentle caress.

She jumped back a foot, startling him. "It's cold!" she blurted out and took another step back. She was rubbing her arms vigorously. "Don't you feel it? It's become quite chilly all of a sudden."

"*Chilly?*" Adam glanced up at the late afternoon sun. *Did she jest?* It was a warm summer's day.

"Yes . . ." She was still rubbing her arms, though her cheeks were pink, indicating inner heat rather than a chilled form. "I could really use your justacorps. Would you mind?"

"No, of course not." Adam removed his overcoat, walked up to her, and placed it on her shoulders.

She shot her arms into the sleeves. On him the coat was knee-length. On her it was much lower. She wrapped her arms around herself, the sleeves too long for her. He could barely see her fingertips.

"Are you all right?" he asked. Her behavior was bizarre.

"Yes . . . No. No, actually, I'm not feeling quite myself. I'm going to lie down until supper. If you'll excuse me . . ." She gave a quick curtsy. "Good-bye," she said as she turned on a heel and stalked away, calling out to her cousin.

Louise d'Arcy abruptly ended her conversation with Robert and raced to Aimee's side, casting a nervous glance Adam's way.

Aimee turned around quickly and tossed out, "I'll return your justacorps later . . . and thank you," then picked up her pace, both women rushing away.

Adam placed his hands on his hips as he watched the hasty retreat.

Robert sauntered over to him, frowning. "What on earth just happened?" he asked.

"I've no idea."

Robert rubbed the back of his neck. "Any reason why is she wearing your justacorps, Adam?"

"She's cold."

Robert lifted a brow. "Cold?"

"That is what I said. Cold."

"*Dieu*, it's about as hot as Hades out here."

Adam watched as the two women entered the palace through one of the garden doors. "Yes. I'm quite aware of that."

Robert shook his head. "It's baffling . . . First there was interest—which is rather astonishing in itself—and then a fast strange exit. What do you suppose is going on?"

"Don't know." It could be that he simply overwhelmed her and she lost her courage. After all, she hadn't been with any other man besides Marc. Or there could be more to this than he knew. "But I do intend to find out." Now that he saw just how responsive she was to him, he was going to continue his pursuit. Adam had a slow seduction in mind for Aimee de Miran.

He wouldn't let her run off the next time. Not until he had her willing and wet and had rocked that edible little body of hers with a powerful release.

*****

"Nothing!" Aimee tossed the blue justacorps onto her bed. "There is absolutely nothing in the pockets." She was so frustrated she wanted to scream. Her body was burning from the inside out, thanks to Adam de Vey—the last man on earth who should stir her. Her husband's friend. A womanizer who had used the very same tactics on countless women.

Those tactics weren't supposed to affect her. But they did. Dear God, had she learned nothing from her experience with Marc? Instead of being the one doing the playing, Aimee was the one being played—by Adam. It unnerved her that he'd incited her senses.

And that he knew it.

"Are you certain?" Louise picked up the coat and ran her hands through the pockets. A sound of exasperation erupted from her as her cousin tossed the justacorps back onto the bed. "We're going to have to search again."

"Oh, no. I'll not go through that again, Louise. We've got to think of something else. Perhaps we can have a jeweler make an identical ring . . . or . . ."

"But that will take too long!" Louise's eyes filled with tears. "Time is of the essence. Renault could realize his ring is missing at any moment."

She knew Louise was right. She was grasping for ideas.

Louise flopped backwards onto the bed. "I'm going to prison." She slapped her palms over her face and wept.

Aimee sighed. Clearly, she was no coquette. Or seductress. She wasn't good at playing the siren. Or the games men like Marc and Adam played. And after her irrational behavior in the gardens, it was almost certain Adam thought she was a lunatic.

But for Louise's sake, she'd have to do better. She knew her cousin would move mountains for her if Aimee were in need. In fact, Louise had been the only one who had been there for her during all the pain Marc had caused her.

"Louise." She walked over to the bed. "You are not going to prison. I'll search his justacorps this evening, providing he wears a blue one, and if that proves fruitless, I'll figure out a way to sneak into his rooms and check all his blue justacorps."

Louise's hands dropped from her face. She sat up immediately. "You will?"

"I will."

She squealed with happiness and leapt off the mattress to give Aimee a tight hug. "Thank you, thank you, thank you."

Despite herself, Aimee smiled. "You're welcome."

Louise pulled away and wiped her tears from her cheeks. "You might want to check his justacorps tonight if he's wearing yellow."

Aimee's smile died. *"Yellow?"*

Louise forced a smile, and taking a step back smoothed her skirts. A bad sign. "Yes, you see . . . I was thinking about when I dropped the ring . . . The Hall of Mirrors was so very crowded.

I was bumped . . . and well . . . he might have been wearing a yellow justacorps."

Aimee simply blinked. Astounded. "How, by all that is holy, can you confuse *blue* with *yellow?*"

"Well . . . It all happened so fast and with the crush of people . . . the truth be told"—she smoothed her skirts again—"I don't recall *exactly* what color he wore."

Aimee strived for patience. For the first time in her life she wanted to throttle her cousin. "Are you even certain that it was Adam de Vey's pocket you dropped the ring in?"

"Oh, yes! Of that I am certain! The man does stand out in a crowd—with his good looks and tall form, although I did find Robert de Senville quite appealing. He is very handsome, and he isn't married. Did you know that?"

"Louise! Focus!"

"Oh, yes, of course. It was *definitely* Adam de Vey. I'm positive. In one of the pockets in one of his justacorps sits Renault's ring. We just have to find out which."

It was like looking for a needle in a haystack given the man's penchant for clothing.

Aimee's every instinct warned her to stay away from the Marquis de Nattes. But she was about to approach . . . and get very close to him, indeed.

A rake who sets your body on fire with the slightest effort . . . Good Lord.

She was going to give this another try.

CHAPTER THREE

Music from violins and harpsichords filled the Hall of Mirrors.

By the time Adam arrived, His Majesty's fete was well under way. Seated on his silver throne at the opposite end of the majestic hall, several carpeted steps high, the King observed those who danced the allemande before him in perfect unison. Onlookers not part of the dancing lined the great mirrored gallery.

Adam spotted Aimee immediately. In a royal blue gown, with a radiant smile on her sweet lips, she danced with grace. He'd looked to the dance floor first, knowing if she were anywhere in the room, he'd likely find her there. Riveted, he watched with pleasure each elegant turn and movement she made. She'd attended many balls with Marc where Adam had caught himself watching her dance. She danced so well, always with that captivating smile that bedazzled him every time.

There was no doubt in his mind—Aimee de Miran was the most beautiful woman in the realm.

Clearly enjoying herself, she made him smile.

He liked seeing her face aglow. Flushed with pleasure. Mental images of her naked in his bed, her soft skin just as pink, just as warm, as he rode her to ecstasy and back, burned through his mind.

His groin tightened.

In all the years he'd known her, he'd never dared to dance with her. He'd never dared touch her while she'd been married to Marc—except to offer her the proper greeting one gave a lady and the wife of a friend. Touching her would only add to his torment, and heighten his desire for a woman who wasn't his to touch.

Without realizing it, Marc had tortured Adam for years with countless details of his wife's beautiful body. He hated it that Marc had discussed his wife with the same level of disregard he had for his paramours.

More than he could ever express.

Though Adam couldn't remember any of the particulars of his friend's many mistresses, he recalled every single detail Marc had mentioned about Aimee's lovely body—when he hadn't wanted to. When he'd wanted nothing more than to forget them. Forget her. Adam knew Aimee had a beauty mark on her inner right thigh and another on her left hip. And he didn't need Marc to tell him just how gorgeous her tits were. He could see that for himself. The top curves of her breasts were presently visible above her décolletage.

And tantalizing in the extreme.

Aimee pressed her palm to her partner's raised hand, and turned in a circle in time with the music and dancers around her. Her dark curls were swept up and adorned with tiny blue ribbons; the few cascading down flounced about—so damned adorably—as she moved. He drank in the sight of her. She was breathtaking to behold.

The only woman he knew who could render him awestruck again and again.

As the last notes were played, she made a final turn and a deep curtsy to her partner, the Baron de Ranvier. Ranvier immediately offered his arm and escorted her off the dance floor.

Intent on intercepting Aimee before she disappeared into the crowd, Adam began to make his way through the throng, just as the King rose, descended the steps, and exited the Hall of Mirrors to enter his gardens.

The crush immediately followed him out, the mass moving across Adam's path making it impossible to do anything but move with the flow.

He lost sight of Aimee.

Moments later, he found himself outside in the gardens. A hush fell over the crowd surrounding him. Anticipation infused the silence as the mass gazed up at the night sky, everyone aware of what was about to happen. Suddenly, the heavens filled with explosions of lights and sounds, spectacular fireworks dazzling and delighting His Majesty's court. Louis did everything on a grand scale to demonstrate to all that he was King of the most powerful realm in all of Christendom. Adam scanned the crowds but couldn't find his golden-eyed beauty.

A hand touched his sleeve and grabbed his attention. To his astonishment, Aimee was standing beside him smiling. His heart quickened, sending blood rushing to his already stiff prick. In an instant, his cock felt as heavy as lead. *Dieu*, this woman had him unbalanced. Each time he thought he'd have to do the chasing, she appeared before him.

Because of the crush around them, she stood so close to him, her soft breasts lightly pressing against his arm, wreaking havoc on his senses.

"Good evening, Adam." Her voice was elevated due to the noise of the fireworks. "Are you enjoying the fireworks?" she asked. He barely noticed them with her so near.

"Yes. Are you?"

Her beautiful golden eyes swept heavenward. "Yes. They're lovely." She returned her gaze to him.

Adam leaned in, using the loudness of the exploding fireworks as his excuse to move closer to her. "I trust you're feeling better?"

"Much better, thank you. How goes the work on the fountains and your machine?"

He smiled, once again pleased by her interest. "It goes well. I'll be giving the King a demonstration tomorrow afternoon."

"Tomorrow? With the keen interest he showed today, I would have thought he'd want to see your demonstration immediately."

"The King has other officials here to meet with. I understand that he was occupied the better part of the day with his Lieutenant General of Police."

Her smile faded slightly. "Oh . . . really? The Lieutenant General of Police . . ." She looked away, gazing up at the skies.

All the telltale signs of her desire were there. Her heart raced; he could see the rapid pulse on her slender neck. And her breathing was a little faster than normal. Someone bumped her from behind, pushing her up against him harder.

A bolt of lust rocked him.

Merde. He had to fuck her. Soon. He couldn't take much more.

She placed a hand against his chest and gently pushed herself away as best she could. "I'm sorry," she said.

"Don't be. I'm not."

To his delight, she didn't shy away. In fact, she hadn't looked all that sorry she'd bumped into him. Her smile was unwavering, bordering on sultry, as she moved to stand in front of him, her skirts deliciously caressing his leg, the space between their bodies so provocatively minimal.

"You're wearing blue," she said, looking pleased.

His gaze drifted down over what he could see of her appealing form. "So are you. Quite magnificently, if the truth be told." He liked the awareness between them.

"I'd say just about any color suits you, Adam. You truly have the finest justacorps."

"Thank you." He'd no idea why they were talking about his clothes except to guess that she was nervous. He could sense it. She wanted to touch him. That much was obvious. As obvious as the heat mounting between them the longer their bodies remained this close.

He definitely approved of the direction this was going . . .

Aimee had stirred his hunger. She could see it in his dark eyes. It was so raw and real, it made her head spin. Clearly, her skill at seduction was improving, for she was the one in command of the game at the moment. All she had to do was remain in control of her desire. And his. *That's how this game is played, no?*

The seducer had command over the seduced.

If only her body wasn't conspiring against her. Being this close to him made her sex slick. And ache. This wasn't about satisfying her starved senses. Or physical longings. This was about helping her cousin and keeping her safe from Renault.

Adam had used women for his own purposes. For his pleasure. She was going use him for hers.

It would give her great pleasure to search his pockets, find the ring, and leave him burning.

Fool. You'll leave yourself burning, too.

She ignored the errant thought. Knowing her own limitations, not wanting to push him or herself too far, lest she got ensnared in her own game, she decided this was a good time to change tactics, demeanor, and tone. Abruptly, she clamped her hands on his shoulders.

"Yes, this is quite a lovely justacorps." She stroked the fabric down his chest, stopping to tap over his breast pockets. No ring in there.

"Wonderful fabric . . . Silk, is it? " She moved her hands farther down the coat, using short strokes in much the same way one would pet a horse. His brow furrowed as he glanced down and watched the odd motions of her hands. *What the bloody hell . . . ?* clearly etched in his expression. She fought to keep a straight face. His expression was priceless. It was obvious he was expecting to be touched in a more amorous way. In perhaps more intimate places on his muscled body.

Aimee refused to dwell on how deliciously solid his chiseled chest felt.

"I just adore silk," she said, then purposely steering well away from his sex, she shot her hands out toward his hips and the pockets there.

He caught her wrists, her hands only inches away from her goal.

"*Chère*, perhaps it's been a long time since you touched a man. Why don't we try something like this?" Before she could react, he pulled her hand inside his justacorps and pressed her palm to the bulge in his breeches. Her heart lurched. Ever so slowly, he stroked her hand down his length, and then back up to the crest of his cock.

A fresh wave of arousal slammed her senses. She lost her breath. He was much thicker and bigger than Marc. And so delectably hard and hot. The most incredible heat emanated from his body through the fine fabric of his breeches.

Her sex responded with a warm gush.

With the crowd so gripped by the entertainment in the skies, she and Adam were cocooned in their small spot, their bodies too close together for anyone to see the wicked motions of their hands over his shaft. Her gaze was locked with his. She couldn't break away, captivated by the passion in his eyes, his fever for her spiking her own.

"That's much better . . ." he murmured, yet somehow she still heard him over the noise.

Her breathing was shallow and sharp. Her clit pulsed fiercely. Aimee curled her fingers tightly around his straining sex inside his tented breeches.

He released her wrist. "Perfect . . ." he murmured, and she realized she was still stroking his glorious cock. As much as it shocked her, she didn't want to let go. Adam slipped his hand behind her neck. He was going to kiss her.

Don't let him! She was teetering on the edge of a complete surrender. Right here. Right now. She'd never been so brazen.

Adam de Vey had masterfully turned the tables on her.

She had wits enough to know when to cede defeat and run. She yanked her hand away from his alluring shaft. "I am feeling a bit chilled." *Get the justacorps and go! Hurry!*

"Chilled?" Amusement flicked in his dark eyes. To her relief, he removed his hand from the nape of her neck. "We can't have that. Allow me to be of assistance." He caught her arm and pulled her to the right until his shoulder met the tall palace wall.

Within the tightly packed throng, their new spot was no less dense with spectators of the King's show of fireworks.

He pulled off his light blue coat. "Turn around, Aimee," he said, slipping the justacorps onto her shoulders the moment she complied.

She slipped her arms into the sleeves and gave him a semblance of a smile over her shoulder as the explosions continued overhead.

He slid his arm inside the justacorps and pulled her up against him. Aimee stiffened. His hard cock was pressed against her bottom. Surely, he wasn't going to do anything more with this crowd around them? Her answer came when she felt her skirts being raised from behind. She sucked in a breath. He was using his hand closest to the wall, using their bodies to hide what he was doing from view. She reeled, stunned by his actions.

"Adam . . ." His name rushed out of her lungs, but the rest of her words were choked off when she felt his hot hand graze over the front of her thigh and cup her sex through the cloth of her drawers. She jumped on contact.

He tightened his arm around her. "Easy . . ." His mouth was against her ear. "Spread your legs for me, Aimee. Let me warm you."

Her heart was hammering. *Warm her?* If she got any hotter, she'd burst into flames. Aimee looked at those closest to them. Did no one notice his hand up her skirts? Heads tilted back and eyes skyward told her definitely "No."

"Your caleçons are wet with your juices. I like that." He rubbed her lightly over her drawers.

Her breathing hitched, and she grabbed the wall, digging her fingers into the stone. The heat from his hand was spine-melting. Her clit throbbed in time with the hard thuds of her heart.

"Do it, *ma belle*. Spread your legs for me. You won't regret it," he coaxed in her ear and lightly bit her earlobe. A sultry sound escaped her mouth. His foot nudged hers. She widened her stance, without another thought, giving him easy access to her needy sex.

"Excellent . . ." His hand had slipped inside the slit of her drawers and he was gently caressing her slick folds, strokes that were all too perfect, inundating her with voluptuous sensations. She whimpered. She'd never done anything like this. So outrageous. So unbridled.

He slid his fingers inside her core. She lurched but his strong arm around her waist kept her in place, not allowing her to escape his delicious invasion. He pumped his hand, the heel of his palm tantalizing her clit. She'd no idea how many of his long wonderful fingers were sliding in and out of her. She knew only a sublime pressure and exquisite friction as he filled her and withdrew. Filled her and withdrew.

"You have the sweetest cunt, Aimee. So wet and silky soft . . . I love how you're squeezing around my fingers. You like being possessed this way, don't you?"

Yes! Shaking, her breaths ragged, she turned her head and pressed her forehead against the back of her hand still clutching the wall, refusing to answer him. Her mind screamed, "End this now!" but she'd no will in her body to stop him. She couldn't even muster a protest when his other hand opened the front of her gown, and pulled down her chemise.

Cool night air whispered through the opening of the justacorps and gently blew across her hardened nipple. A soft cry slipped past her lips.

He captured the distended tip of her breast and masterfully rolled and pinched it. She could barely hold in the sounds surging up her throat.

"Have you ever been fingered like this in public, Aimee?"

She shook her head. Her husband had never done anything like this to her. Had never incited her to this magnitude. Her muscles were taut. Her body tensed as she fought against the waves of hot lust crashing through her, wrestling for a modicum of control.

"*Chère*, don't fight it. Let me give you the pleasure your body is hungry for . . . You want to come, don't you, beautiful Aimee?"

She was panting now, yet she managed to nod her head. What was the point in denying it? He was purposely holding her on the edge with his skillful hands and measured strokes. He could send her over the edge anytime he wanted.

"Let me hear you say—"

"I want to come!" she quickly injected before he could finish his sentence. "Now! Right now . . ." She didn't care if someone heard her. Or where she was. She needed this. Needed him. Wanted what he was offering. Had to have it or die.

"I want to come for you, Adam." She heard the smile in his tone as he fed her the line in her ear, his experienced hands holding her gripped in a flood of erotic sensations.

"Yes . . . I want to come . . ." Squeezing her eyes shut, she was practically delirious with desire.

". . . for you, Adam," he supplied.

". . . I want to come for you . . . Adam."

He kissed her neck, trailing his way to the sensitive spot below her ear. "It would be an honor to pleasure you, Aimee . . ." Curling his buried fingers, he brushed over the ultrasensitive spot inside her vaginal wall.

A cry burst from her lips, her knees almost giving way as he stroked that sweet spot with stunning finesse, milking more juices from her sex. Her hips jerked forward. Her sex contracted, and she knew she was going to go over soon. Very soon. The pleasure and tension inundating her became entwined into one exquisite sensation, mountaining inside her. Surging fast. And furious.

His name erupted from her mouth. Rapture exploded through her senses, her body stiffening. She pushed up against him hard, her scream eclipsed by the final firecrackers in the sky, her sheath contracting wildly around his fingers.

"That's it, Aimee. Ride it out. I've got you." He held her, his strokes slowing down only when the delicious spasms ebbed.

Applause burst around her, signaling the end of the fireworks display.

Adam slid his fingers out, the luscious sense of fullness slipping away. She shivered. Her skirts fell back in place while he busied his other hand with her bodice. Knowing people were about to leave, she tried to help, her trembling fingers fumbling, hindering his progress.

"Let me," he said softly in her ear. In short order, he had the front of her gown closed without anyone around them being the wiser.

She turned and slumped against the wall, still wearing his justacorps as the crowd disbursed toward the tables set out in the gardens for the feast about to be served. Her breathing and heart calmed. She felt euphoric, her muscles deliciously lax.

She felt light enough to fly.

Her marital relations with Marc had been the best part of their marriage, and as good as they were, they had never been like this. She'd never been left feeling this incredible. There was a wonderful warmth in her belly that was slowly seeping through her entire being. A calm sated feeling. A feeling of well-being. A peace.

She met his gaze. The night's light shone on one side of his handsome face, making him look even more devilishly beautiful. He was beyond potent. Dangerously irresistible. Women throughout the realm should be warned—the Marquis de Nattes had devastating allure and sexual talents no mortal man should possess.

He ran a knuckle lightly down her cheek. It was then she realized it was wet. Oh God . . . He'd moved her to tears during sex. She swiped her other cheek dry, embarrassed by the unprecedented occurrence. She'd made it a habit of hiding her tears during her marriage. Never once had she shown them to Marc.

"You come beautifully, Aimee."

How did one answer that? "Thank you"?

Most of the crowd was gone. They were all but alone. Did he expect pleasure in return? Of course he did. Marc demanded pleasure for pleasure. Didn't all men?

A sudden urge to taste him swelled inside her. She quashed it. "I . . . should go." She expected his ire to hit at any moment. Yet, it was the only response she could offer. She desperately needed some distance to collect herself. To snap this unsettling spell he'd cast on her.

The corner of his perfect mouth lifted in the most sensual smile. "If you must."

No anger?

"My cousin awaits me," she told him, completely unsure why.

He took a step back. "Then you shouldn't keep her waiting."

She shouldn't? No argument? He was simply letting her go after giving her the strongest orgasm of her life?

She held his gaze, unsure what more to say. His expression was unreadable and she wished she knew what he was thinking.

She pushed herself off the wall. "All right then." She managed a smile, feeling out of sorts, unable to shake the wish that he'd demand more of her. A kiss. Or simply to give that delectable part of his male anatomy that was still solid and erect some carnal attention.

If he's this talented with his hands, imagine what he can do with that beautiful cock.

She immediately chastised herself. *Those sorts of thoughts will get you into the kind of trouble you don't need.*

"Are you sufficiently warmed now?" he asked.

"Pardon? Oh, yes, I . . . I'm warm now." *Warm me some more . . .*

"Then may I have my justacorps?"

Her brows shot up. "Oh, of course . . ." It suddenly occurred to her she'd never checked the lower pockets. She'd completely forgotten to search for the ring. Aimee drove her hands into the pockets and brightened her smile. "This really is a very nice justacorps." She slid her fingers around the pockets, hoping to touch upon the ring. "You do have exquisite taste in clothing."

"Thank you." He looked amused. "The justacorps, if you please?"

Nothing. The pockets were empty. "Yes . . . absolutely. Here." She removed the coat and handed it to him.

He leisurely put it on. She watched with fascination as one strong shoulder and then the other slipped inside the blue knee-length coat. In the distance she could hear the chatter of the courtiers and strains from the violins.

His dark eyes gazed back at her but he said nothing more. *Why are you still standing here, Aimee? Leave!* "Good evening, Adam."

"Good evening, Aimee."

She took a step, then stopped and said, "Thank you." *Thank you? Good God. Did you just thank him for giving you a climax?* She felt her face turn red. One release and she was behaving like an unsophisticated fool.

His lips twitched and she could tell he was holding back a smile. "For what?"

The devil. He knew full well what she'd just thanked him for. He was going to make her spell it out. "For the . . . uhm . . . the . . ."

"Orgasm?" he supplied.

She was grateful it was night and he couldn't see just how red her cheeks were. "Yes, for . . . that."

A slow steady smile graced his mouth, one of pure male pride. "It was my pleasure."

Oh, he was good. Much better than Marc on too many disquieting levels.

She gave a nod and, feeling completely awkward, forced one foot in front of the other, walking away from Adam, tamping down the desire to rush back to him. The sight of Renault de Sard, Louise's former lover, marching toward her stopped her dead in her tracks.

"I want a word with you," he said the moment he reached her.

"Really? I don't much care to have one with you, sir," Aimee bit back. The wonderful lassitude that had been humming in her veins dissipated instantly by Renault's presence.

"Have you seen your cousin?" He was unfazed by her curtness.

"Of course I've seen her. I see her quite regularly." She stepped around him.

"Halt right there," Renault ordered.

Aimee turned around to see Adam approaching, a frown furrowing his handsome brow.

"I've not dismissed you," Renault added.

Aimee set her jaw. "I don't need your dismissal to leave your presence, sir."

Renault walked up to her. "I am the King's Lieutenant General of Police."

"So?"

"So I am permitted to detain anyone I choose and ask them questions."

Aimee's ire heated her blood. "Do you dare speak to me as if I were a criminal? Have you forgotten your place?" She never threw her title or social standing around for clout, but he'd been made noble because of his political office.

She was a noble by blood. And, after the way he'd treated her cousin, he deserved a dressing-down.

"What is the problem, Renault?" Adam placed his hand on the vermin's shoulder.

She disliked everything about the man. His arrogance. His cutting disregard of Louise and her affections. She never understood what her dear cousin saw in him. About the same age as Adam, Renault was of similar coloring, yet of slighter build. And his features were as stern as his disposition.

Upon seeing Adam, Renault changed his demeanor. "Oh, it's you, Nattes. It's nothing . . . Just a matter between a former mistress and me."

Adam looked at Aimee and lifted a brow.

She immediately added, "He's referring to my cousin. A lovely woman with terrible taste in men." She looked pointedly at Renault. The last thing she wanted was for Adam—or anyone—to think she'd take a lover as unappealing as Renault de Sard.

"Your 'lovely' cousin has never behaved herself a single day I've known her, yet she has stayed away as requested and not a peep has been heard from her," Renault said. "A most uncharacteristic behavior. I want to know why. What is she up to? It's usually no good."

"Perhaps she's finally come to the conclusion that you are a waste of her time," she responded, coolly.

With that, Aimee picked up her skirts, turned on her heel, and stalked away on weak and wobbly legs, her heart pounding. That was all she needed—for Renault to be keeping Louise under close scrutiny.

Reaching the long elegant tables with gold service, surrounded by torchères, Aimee scanned the area and quickly located Louise. She was by her side in an instant.

"Where have you been, Aimee?" Louise whispered the moment Aimee sat down. "I've been looking for you everywhere."

"I got caught up in the crowd," she responded vaguely, not quite ready to talk about her encounter with Adam.

"Did you find Adam de Vey?"

Just as Aimee was about to respond, she glanced down the lengthy table and caught Adam's gaze. He was seated at the same table at the opposite end. He smiled at her and lightly ran the length of his finger along his upper lip, just under his nose.

Heat rushed to her cheeks as the impact of what he was doing hit her. Her scent was on his fingers, and he was clearly enjoying it. She felt a quickening low in her belly. Her sex clenched, hungrily.

She tore her gaze away and forced her focus onto Louise.

"Oh, look, Aimee. Adam de Vey is at our table." Once again, Louise pointed out the obvious. "Do you want to check his justacorps?"

"No!" she cringed at how strongly that came out. "I mean, I already did, darling. There was no ring."

Louise's disappointment was etched across her features.

"That's not all, Louise." Aimee covered her hand affectionately. "Renault is suspicious of you and thinks you're up to something."

Louise flinched. "Oh God! He does?"

"Yes, I think I defused it some, but we must be careful. And we must act quickly." Aimee glanced down the table, but found the beautiful Marquis de Nattes gone. His seat had been vacated and another sat in his place.

Disappointment over his disappearance stabbed into her. And irked her.

Her unusual behavior toward him was completely explainable. Her lengthy celibacy was to blame, motivating her wanton reactions to him. Nothing more.

"Tomorrow afternoon the Marquis de Nattes has a meeting with the King."

Louise's eyes widened. "And?"

"And I intend to go to his personal apartments and check in each and every justacorps he owns until I find the ring."

All this madness was going to end tomorrow.

CHAPTER FOUR

"You can stop grinning like a fool, Robert," Adam said dryly. Palms pressed against the large desk in the King's private apartments, studying his drawings while waiting for His Majesty to arrive, Adam could see his friend out of the corner of his eye.

"You're being very quiet about your whereabouts last night." Robert was smirking. "And as coincidence would have it, last night Louise d'Arcy couldn't locate her cousin anywhere. She came to me and asked if I'd seen her. Any idea where the fair Aimee de Miran was last eve?"

Adam felt his cock harden at the mention of Aimee and last night. *Merde.* A stiff prick was the last thing he needed just before he met with the King. Damn Robert.

The memory of Aimee in his arms, of her honeyed sex squeezing around his fingers while she came, rushed through his mind. That very same memory had kept him up most of the night—keeping both him and his cock fully awake.

Adam had always enjoyed a chase—especially since he didn't usually get much resistance to his advances, but his pursuit of Aimee was far more than mere entertainment. Having her meant too much to him.

More than it should.

More than he was comfortable with. His desire for her had spanned an eternity. Nothing had been so difficult as to watch her walk away last eve and not pull her back and claim what she so obviously wanted him to take.

But he refused to do it and resisted by sheer iron will.

If she wanted to be taken, she was going to have to come to him and ask with her very own sweet lips—without reservation or inhibitions. To that end, he'd made great strides last eve, despite being left with a painful prick. She'd lingered afterward, waiting for him to demand more, and the disappointment in her golden eyes when he hadn't had been difficult to miss.

Adam sensed it wasn't going to take much longer. Then she'd be all his.

And he had six years of pent-up fantasies to indulge in with her.

Robert walked over smiling, and stopping on the opposite side of the desk, pressed his palms down onto the surface. "Please tell me you fucked her. Any man who's been walking around with a stiff cock for another man's wife for six years deserves some relief."

Adam looked him square in the eye, grasping for patience with his irksome friend. "Remind me again why I tolerate you?"

Robert laughed and straightened. "You've got that wrong. I tolerate *you*," he teased. "What happened with Aimee? Out with it."

Adam pushed himself off the desk and blew out a breath. "Robert, she's never had a lover." Of that he was certain. Since Marc's death, he'd kept his ears open, always listening for news about her.

While in mourning she'd kept mostly to herself at her country château, her main company, her cousin Louise. But once the mourning was over, she'd returned to Paris. Adam knew whenever she was in the city and he'd made it a point of attending those salons and fetes she'd be at. He'd kept his distance, sensing the timing wasn't right, sensing she wasn't ready to take a lover—though controlling his gaze whenever she was in the room was a different challenge altogether.

"If I push for too much too soon, she'll bolt." He was approaching this the way he'd approach any challenge, methodically, carefully, with well-thought-out steps.

"So you didn't bed her."

"Not exactly."

"Not exactly?"

"It was more of a sampling."

"You *sampled* her?" Robert burst out laughing.

Adam rested his hands on his hips. "What about that amuses you?"

Robert shook his head, still chuckling. "Nattes, you are either losing your touch, or you have the worst *tendre* for this woman. Which is it, my friend? I'm starting to strongly suspect it's the latter."

"Don't be ridiculous. Once I have her, the fascination will be over." Adam instantly quashed the doubts that assailed him. He had this under control.

Last night was a perfect example how he had mastery over himself.

"Well, it's fortuitous that the King has moved our meeting up. By the time we're done here, it should be midday. You'll have the entire afternoon and evening free to find the lovely Comtesse de Gremont and break your 'fascination' with her."

True enough. The moment his morning meeting with His Majesty was over, he planned to return to his rooms, refresh himself, and seek Aimee out.

She didn't know about his change of plans and thought he'd be occupied most of the afternoon with the King.

He couldn't wait to surprise her.

*****

Aimee's heart pounded as she approached the doors to Adam's apartments. She couldn't believe she was doing something like this. For the last three years, her life had been a staid, quiet existence. Stealing into a man's rooms was much more adventure than she'd ever known.

Or ever wanted to know.

In truth, her entire visit to the palace had been one unprecedented experience after another.

There were so many apartments at the palace—housed in the various outbuildings—that it had been quite the chore simply learning where Adam's rooms were located. She'd been forced to make careful, discreet inquiries.

Fearing she'd be seen in the corridor by someone she knew, Aimee picked up her pace and rushed to the door. The last thing she wanted was to be questioned about being in an outbuilding that was not where her apartments were located. Or even close to it.

Standing before Adam's door, she paused, her left hand clutching his justacorps in a white-knuckle grip. If caught by a servant, she'd simply say she was returning the Marquis's overcoat that she'd borrowed the first day she'd arrived—because she was *cold*.

In the middle of a hot summer's day.

Most definitely a weak and sorry excuse, Aimee.

Sadly, it was the best she could come up with at the time.

Taking a deep breath, she exhaled slowly. She was doing this alone. Louise was so nervous, she'd trembled and babbled uncontrollably, leaving no doubt in Aimee's mind that her cousin would have foiled the plan.

Get on with it. You can't stand here staring at the door all afternoon.

Aimee raised a shaky hand and lightly rapped at the door.

Silence. *Excellent!*

Placing a hand on the door handle, she turned it and opened the portal, her heart galloping wildly. A quick peek told her no one was in the antechamber. She slipped inside and closed the door softly.

Aimee looked around the elegant room. White and gilded walls. Tall windows overlooking the gardens, and two doors. One ajar. The other closed. Approaching the open door, she could see it led to the bedchambers, the floral-patterned rugs on the floor muting her footsteps.

However, nothing quieted the thundering of her heart. It was so loud in her ears, next to the stillness surrounding her.

Entering Adam's bedchamber, she couldn't miss the massive four-poster bed with its blue counterpane and matching bed curtains. Seeing it made her insides dance and conjured up heated images of last night in her mind.

This was not the time to think about *that*.

Pulling her gaze away from Adam's bed, she glanced to the right and spotted exactly what she was looking for.

Two large ornately carved armoires.

This would be so much easier if the man hadn't had the amount of clothing that required a second armoire.

She walked to the closest one and opened its doors. Numerous suits of clothing, in various colors, were folded and stacked high in neat piles. Throwing open the doors to the second armoire, she found it just as overflowing with clothing. My God. It was going to take hours to unfold, search, and refold each justacorps and return it to its spot.

Frustrated, Aimee cast a glance heavenward, needing a miracle. *Why couldn't it be as simple as reaching in*—she shoved a hand in to one of the piles—*and pulling out the ring?* As she was sliding her hand back out, her fingers stroked over something small and hard inside a pocket.

The ring!

"May I help you?" A male voice made her jump, tear her hand out of the pile, and spin around.

Her knees almost buckled when she saw Adam leaning against the doorframe wearing nothing but a bath linen around his waist.

Utterly absorbed, she moved her gaze over his magnificent sculpted chest, devouring each beautiful dip and ripple. He was nothing short of pure masculine perfection. She watched the gorgeous flex of his bicep as he raised his hand and ran it through his wet dark hair before crossing his strong arms over that powerful chest.

Gracious God . . . As handsome as her husband had been, he'd never looked like *that*.

"What are you doing here, Aimee?"

Stop ogling him.

She tore her eyes away and glanced back at the armoire. Her heart plummeted the moment she realized she couldn't remember which pile she'd stuck her hand in, or the color of the justacorps she'd been touching in the stack.

"Aimee, I asked you a question."

Her gaze shot back to him. She quickly averted it when she got another eyeful of his glorious—mostly naked—physique.

"I came to return this." She held her arm out, the justacorps she was holding now dangling from her grip, purposely blocking the sight of him. "I was . . . going to place it back in your armoire. I didn't know you were here. I am sorry to have interrupted you. You're clearly busy. I'll go."

She placed the justacorps down on his bed and, with her heart pounding in her throat, turned to leave.

"Aimee, come here."

That arrested her steps. His voice was low and so wickedly sensual. She had to swallow hard before she could speak, her insides frenzied—a dizzying combination of dread and something else she didn't want to name.

"That's probably not a good idea," she said without turning around. Waving her hand in his direction behind her, she added, "You'll want to get dressed, lest you catch a chill."

"It's a warm summer's day outside and it's quite pleasant in here. I'm not in the least bit cold. Are you chilled, Aimee? Do you need warming—"

"*No!*" She winced, not intending the word to be dealt so abruptly. "No . . . I'm fine . . . Warm enough, thank you." *Get out now or you'll end up being warmed in ways best avoided.* As it was, the sight of him was already heating her blood.

"Come over here, Aimee," he repeated. By his tone, it was clear he was insisting.

Did she have a choice? Adam and Renault were friends, and they were both in the King's inner circle. She had to get out of this situation as smoothly as she could.

Which meant she couldn't bolt out the door as she wanted.

Keeping her eyes averted, she turned around and approached him, praying he couldn't tell just how discomposed she was.

She stood before him and purposely kept her gaze fixed to the wall past his shoulder. She clasped her hands in front of her, then quickly unclasped them, realizing she'd brought her hands near that particular part of his male anatomy. The one covered by the bath linen she was trying not to think about. Or peek at.

He slipped his fingers under her chin and tilted her face, forcing her to meet his gaze. "What are you doing in my bedchambers, Aimee?"

"I told you. I wanted to return the justacorps . . ."

He gripped her shoulders and pressed her back against the wall, surprising her with his actions. Bracing his hands on either side of her head, he dipped his head, bringing his handsome face closer—his body hemming her in. "Why don't you try again."

"Try again?" she asked.

"With a better answer. One that's honest."

Her heart lurched. Aimee forced herself to look him firmly in the eye.

"I was returning the justacorps," she insisted. Could he hear her pounding heart? How she wished he had on clothes. The lack of which was making this entire episode even more distressing. His skin was driving her to distraction. It looked warm and inviting as it covered all that impressive muscle and sinew.

"Aimee, you have servants. There is no need for you to come here, unless you had a reason for wanting to be in my bedchambers yourself."

She didn't like the direction this conversation was taking. Unsettled, she wanted out of his chambers. Right now.

"You have my answer. This discussion is over." Her response was sharp.

He blew out a breath. "I'm not trying to upset you. I simply want to hear the truth from your beautiful mouth." He pulled a hand away from the wall and lightly brushed his fingertips across her bottom lip. Leaving a tingling in its wake. "*Dieu*, I have fantasized about this mouth, your sweet form . . . you . . . for a very long time."

That, too, took her by surprise.

He ran the back of his fingers gently down her cheek, the side of her neck, and onto the swells of her breasts. Her breathing quickened. Ever so slowly, his fingers grazed her skin, following the contour of her décolletage, his soft touch sending her nerve endings into a frenzy, making her nipples harden and her sex slick. "I enjoyed making you come last night. I only wish I'd seen your face when you came . . . And as for these lovely breasts, I still don't know the exact shade of your nipples."

He stroked the tip of his finger down the front of her gown, directly over one distended tip. She gasped, the sensation intense, despite the clothing. "I've lost count how many times I imagined touching you. Tasting you. In my mind, I have fucked you a thousand times." He cupped her breast and caressed her nipple with his thumb, the rhythmic strokes making her shiver in delight. "That is honest. That is the truth. Now I want the truth from you. Why did you come into my chambers? I know you feel the heat between us. Admit that you want me as much as I want you."

Oh God. And here she thought she'd stirred his suspicions. She'd no idea that *desire* was the truth he wanted to hear—to admit to the hunger he incited in her. Nor did she have any idea he'd desire her "for a very long time."

"I didn't know that you have—"

"Wanted you for years?" He shrugged. "You were married to Marc and he had your affections. Why let it be known?"

Years? "How many years?"

"From the moment I first saw you."

Six years? She wanted to discount what he was saying, to believe it was just the kind of lie a libertine would tell a woman he wanted to bed, but there was such touching sincerity in his dark eyes, she couldn't dismiss it, no matter how much she wished to.

When Marc had stopped wanting her, stopped touching her, and left her feeling undesirable and empty, Adam de Vey had wanted her. From a distance he'd craved her—*for six years* . . . It was stunning. *Incredible* . . . Unbelievably stirring.

"This is our time, Aimee. I want to share more carnal pleasures with you, but first I'm going to need to hear from your lips that you want it. That the reason you came to my rooms is because you're hungry for what I can give you."

With his thumb lightly tormenting her nipple, she could barely think. He had her cornered into quite a predicament. If she denied her desire for him, then she'd have to convince him that her original excuse for being in his rooms was the truth.

The problem was, she didn't want to deny her desire. Every fiber of her being wanted him with shocking desperation. Wanted to tell him the truth on that score.

He dipped his dark head and brushed his mouth over the sensitive spot below her ear; a frisson of excitement quivered through her. "Last night, while you were lying in bed, did you think of me?" His warm breath caressed her ear.

She licked her lips, starved for his taste. "Yes . . ." she whispered.

"Did you imagine me in your bed with you?"

Her core clenched. "Yes."

He nuzzled her neck. "Did you imagine my cock inside you, Aimee? Did you imagine me fucking you?"

He was trailing knee-weakening kisses down her neck. Briefly she closed her eyes, the sensations so decadent. She'd never had a conversation like this in her life. She would have been too embarrassed to tell Marc about any sexual thoughts she'd had, but with Adam the words slipped past her lips with ease. "*Yes* . . ."

"I'm pleased to hear that." She could hear the smile in his tone. "Last night, I thought about you, too. I thought about that perfect sweet sex of yours and how delicious that slick, snug heat would feel around my cock." He pulled back, looked into her eyes, and slipped his fingers under her chin. He tilted it up, bringing her lips so temptingly close to his seductive mouth. "It seems we are of like mind," he murmured, then swooped in for a kiss, his tongue possessing her mouth immediately. She all but swooned. The intensity of his kiss was inebriating.

She wanted to touch him so strongly—but hesitated. This man was far too devastating on her famished senses. He had the uncanny ability to arouse her to a feverish pitch and had her saying and doing things she'd never said or done before. Last eve he'd driven her so wild, she'd allowed him to have shocking liberties and in a public place—the palace gardens surrounded by the King's court. Everyone knew her as a dutiful wife and at present a respectable widow. Yet in *his* arms, she was uninhibited and undone.

Aimee pressed her palms to the wall behind her back, but let the delicious fire emanating from Adam burn through her, unable to help herself.

By the time he broke the kiss, she was utterly breathless.

Desperate for more.

"Tell me, Aimee, are you here to give yourself to me?"

CHAPTER FIVE

All right, perhaps it wasn't the real reason Aimee had entered Adam's chambers. But Lord knows she wanted to give herself to him. Again. The bud between her legs pulsed fiercely and her sex, soaked with her juices, ached to be filled. By Adam de Vey. She never thought she'd ever desire another man as much as she'd desired Marc.

She desired Adam more. With a reckless abandon she didn't know she was capable of.

Why couldn't she help her cousin *and* enjoy Adam's sexual skills? The last few years had been devoid of joy. Why deny herself some pleasure? This man knew how to give it in wicked abundance.

"Answer me, *chère*. Did you come here to give yourself to me?" His sinfully seductive eyes were locked with hers, waiting for her response.

"Yes" tripped off her tongue.

He smiled, clearly pleased by her response. "Open the front of your gown and offer me your nipples."

Hot excitement melted down her spine. Everything he said to her was so deliciously carnal. It amazed her how much she liked it. Marc had never spoken to her like this in or out of the bedchamber.

Without another thought, her fingers flew to her bodice, opening the fastenings. Her nipples were so hard, she couldn't stand having them confined any longer. Bracing his palms against the wall, he watched, patient yet hungry. She yanked at her clothing, pulled at her stays, her fingers fumbling a bit, until she reached her chemise. Grabbing its lace neckline, she pulled it down, revealing herself, and tucked the neckline under her breasts.

Her breathing sharp and shallow, she watched as he took her in. Her body so eager, it trembled with anticipation.

"You're even more beautiful than I imagined," he breathed. She felt a quickening in her belly. His palms were still pressed to the wall. How she wanted his hands to be on her. "Tell me, Aimee, what is it you want me to do to these pretty pink nipples?"

Her head fell back against the wall. It was getting more and more difficult not to squirm and beg. "Whatever you want."

The look in his eyes darkened immediately, almost as though a feral need rolled through him. Softly he swore. "I like your answer . . . very much." He lowered his head. She braced herself for the thrill of his mouth.

He swirled his tongue around the sensitive tip of her breast. She squeezed her eyes shut, mentally willing him to take her into his mouth. He then sucked her nipple in, wet heat closing around her, tearing a cry from her throat. Her hips jerked forward, her fingers tangling in his hair, pulling him tightly against her.

He released her nipple in an instant. Gently grasping her wrists, he lowered her arms to her sides, the corner of his mouth lifting, giving her his usual seductive smile. "Your responses are delicious. But I want you to stay just like that. Arms down. For now, the only touching I want is my mouth on your body. I've waited so damned long to have you. I'm going to savor you."

He dipped his head and sucked the sensitized nipple back into his hot mouth. A whimper shot up her throat. If she thought he was extraordinarily talented with his hands, he was even more so with his mouth. He had her digging her fingers into the wall, practically clawing at it as he lightly bit and suckled her. Each perfect pull of his mouth made her clit throb.

Adam turned to her other breast and assailed it with the same sweet torment.

He loved it that she couldn't stop the erotic rocking of her hips. That she couldn't take her eyes off him, utterly enthralled as she watched his mouth on her breast. Her reactions were unrestrained and so sensual. She was even more luscious than he'd imagined.

This was far better than anything he'd imagined in his wildest dreams. Nothing compared to actually tasting and touching this woman. The very woman who'd invaded too many of his dreams and waking thoughts.

His heart hammered against his ribs.

He was really going to have Aimee de Miran. This was no dream. It was real.

His golden-eyed siren was before him and his for the taking.

The mere notion made his cock thicker and harder. Made the tip of his prick seep spunk. His sac was so full, it ached.

"Please . . . Adam . . ."

Jésus-Christ. Every time she said his name, a jolt of lust shot through him.

Releasing her pebbled teat from his mouth, he pulled back to admire the pretty bud.

"Please what, Aimee?" He gave her nipple a pinch, enjoying the sensuous mewl she made.

"I can't . . . take any more." She was visibly trembling against the wall.

"Tell me what you want. Let me hear it." He'd waited forever for the words. For this moment. For her.

"I want . . . to kiss you . . .and . . . to touch you, Adam."

That wasn't exactly what he expected to hear, but then just about anything from her mouth sent him up in flames. *Dieu*, she was as endearing as she was arousing.

"Come here and do it, then," he said, his voice rough with desire.

She pushed herself off the wall and stepped close. Her soft hands cupped his face and she pressed her warm mouth to his.

Adam parted his lips, a silent demand for her to slip her tongue inside his mouth. She complied in an instant, lavishing his tongue with soft swirling caresses, a kiss that was so tender it leveled him. At the height of passion, when the fire burned this hot, he hadn't anticipated being at the receiving end of anything this gentle.

His groin tightened as did his heart.

He was suddenly flooded with soft emotions he didn't ordinarily experience during sex.

Unsettled, he pulled her to him, her soft breasts colliding against his chest, intent on keeping this on familiar ground. The way he preferred it—sex that was raw and recreational. Without emotions involved. Love was for poets. He was a man of science. He was governed by logic. Reason. He wasn't ruled by emotion. He didn't fall in love. He fell in and out of lust.

A sultry sound escaped her. She slipped an arm around his neck while her other hand still cupped his cheek, and she caressed the side of his face with the softest stroke.

He pushed her up against the wall and took charge of the kiss, his tongue possessing her mouth as his hands busied themselves with the fastenings on her clothing. Forget savoring. He was moving straight to fucking. He had to sate this unfed hunger—once and for all. To silence the maddening ways she made him feel.

His practiced hands discarded her clothing and had her quickly down to her chemise.

Removing the knee-length garment off her, he swept her up in his arms and, walking up to the bed, dropped her in the middle of it. She landed with her legs sprawled. Her breasts giving a luscious little jiggle.

Having stripped off her garments, all he'd left on her were her drawers. On her back, her pretty tits rising and falling with her rapid breaths, she watched him intently. Adam grabbed the ties at her waist, pulled them loose, and yanked the drawers off. His breath lodged in his throat.

She had mouthwatering curves, the softest-looking skin, and the most adorable belly he'd ever seen. She was beyond beautiful. She was perfection.

Better than any man had a right to.

"Spread your legs wider." His impatience to have her resonated in his tone. His words came out sharper than he intended.

His breaths dragging in and out of his lungs, he watched as she did what he asked. There, on the inside of her right thigh and on her left hip were the beauty marks he'd heard about.

They were even prettier than he'd pictured.

Adam tossed off his bath linen and sank his knees into the mattress between her opened thighs, his cock throbbing and eager. Her glistening sex now had his rapt attention. He'd intended on savoring that sweet sex until she came against his mouth, but he had to bury his cock inside her. Or lose his mind.

And yet, with urgency pounding in his veins, with his cock hard and heavy, he couldn't resist a small sampling of her sex. Especially that edible little clit, so swollen with need. A delectable offering he simply couldn't deny himself. He lowered his mouth onto the sensitive bud and gave it a light suck, sending her arching off the bed with a cry. With a soft teasing lick along her folds and over her clit, he straightened and was back to kneeling between those gorgeous legs. Her taste on his tongue spiked his hunger.

Heavily panting, she held his gaze.

"You're delicious, Aimee. There will be more of that next time. Right now, I'm going to fuck you," he said.

She sat up. Before he knew what she was about, she clasped her hand around the base of his shaft and sucked the head of his cock into her hot wet mouth. A growl shot out of him, his eyes practically rolling back in his head as she milked a dollop of pre-come out of his prick and into her mouth. Slowly, she drew him back out, licked the tip and then her lips, leaving his cock throbbing harder, rioting for more.

Rising up onto her knees, she wrapped her arms around his neck. "You're delicious," she whispered near his mouth. "There will be more of that next time. Right now, I want you to . . . to . . .fuck me, Adam."

Merde. If he could smile, he would. There weren't a lot of women who could turn the tables on him. And in such a delicious way.

He should have known bright and beautiful Aimee would be different.

One simple suck from her mouth left him shaky.

She leaned in and Adam knew she was about to deliver another of her heart-stirring, mind-bending kisses.

He had her down on her back on the bed in an instant, his body covering hers, making her squeak in surprise. Staring into her eyes, he took her wrists and slowly raised her arms above her head, pinning them there. Her eyes widened, but she did not fight him.

"I'm not going to be gentle," he warned, his knees spreading her legs wide. He had six years of pent-up hunger to purge.

She shivered. "I don't care."

"I'm going to take you fast and hard. Then, I'm going to have you again and ride you slow and deep." He brushed his mouth along her jaw and down her throat. She was so silky soft everywhere. Having her naked and against him was indescribable bliss. Still holding her wrists pinned to the mattress, he said. "You're going to come for me all afternoon and night."

She was panting and squirming, impatient, but his body held her relatively still. "Yes. I want that . . . I want . . .*Oh!*"

He firmly jabbed his engorged prick against her opening, intentionally making her gasp. "What do you want, Aimee?" The urge to drive his cock into her wet heat was near overwhelming.

"I want your beautiful . . . c-cock." It was adorable how she stumbled over the more indelicate words each time, telling him this wasn't normal bedroom talk for her. Clearly, she hadn't done this with Marc, and that pleased him, more than he'd ever admit.

Adam thrust the crest of his cock inside her and froze, a guttural groan rumbling out of him. Hot silk was clenched around him. She was tight. So gloriously tight. His heart slammed wildly against his ribs. He had to bury his entire length in her. *Right now.* Retreating slightly, he drove into the most heavenly cunt he'd ever known. She cried out and arched, sucking him in a fraction deeper.

Adam wanted to howl with bliss.

He had his siren nailed to the mattress, his cock buried to the hilt. His mind, body, and soul reveled. At last . . . she was his. And she felt incredible; her snug grip on him was nothing short of spine-melting pleasure.

All the years he'd hungered for her was worth *this.* She was worth the wait.

Their chests heaved as he started down at her lovely face. Her eyes were shut. Her head was turned, her quickened breaths warming his arm. A single tear slipped out the corner of her eye.

"Are you all right?" he croaked out.

She met his gaze. "Yes . . . You feel so good inside me." Those words and the sweet way she'd uttered them constricted his heart. "Please, Adam, let me touch you . . ."

Her kiss and touch had a potent effect on him. His every instinct warned him not to release his hold on her wrists, to maintain a level of distance, to keep this more sexual than personal, but the next thing he knew, he'd let go and she was drawing her arms around him, then her legs, her heels digging deliciously into the small of his back.

And nothing, *nothing* in his life had ever felt better than having Aimee wrapped around him, her warm soft hands moving over his shoulders. Caressing his back. Pressing hot kisses along his neck. He closed his eyes, basking in the sensations. In her.

"I want to come for you, Adam," she whispered against his skin.

He swore. Then reared and plunged, reared and plunged, quickly picking up the pace, driving his cock into the softness of her sex, deep and hard, fucking her with all his strength. She was going to come for him, all right. She was going to come on his cock. Harder than she'd ever come in her life. For every plunge and drag the friction was stunning. It seemed every sensation was intensified with her. He knew he was headed toward his own powerful release.

Adam caught her face between his hands and claimed her mouth in a ravenous kiss as he continued ramming her, enjoying the mews she made against his mouth with each deep thrust. His mind no longer ruled his body. He was completely engulfed in the unsated desire he had for her. She tried rocking her hips, but she was pinned under him, unable to do more than take his driving thrusts.

A bead of sweat rolled down his back. He was reeling in the moment. He wasn't just fucking a woman. This was *the* woman. His golden-eyed temptress. His angel and tormentor. Possessing her. Claiming her. Her body surrendering to him.

Her slick walls clenched down around him, sending a wicked jolt through him. Stealing his breath away. He could tell she was about to fly over the edge. His semen surged in his sac.

The urge to spend was almost more than he could take. He'd never had to fight so hard to control his climax the way he had to with her. "Give me what I want, *Aimee*. Come for me."

Her body stiffened. Her slick walls tightened. Then she screamed, her feminine muscles contracting along his plunging length, snatching a groan from his throat.

He was shaking, thrusting, holding on to the load of come he was dying to discharge, just so he could ride her longer. Not wanting to leave her sweet form. Not wanting this moment, this experience with *this* woman to end.

His control frayed until it finally snapped. Hot come came barreling down his cock. He reared just as semen spewed out of him and onto her belly. He threw back his head and roared her name, gripped by the paralyzing pleasure flooding through him. Come purged from his prick in forceful blasts until at last he'd emptied his cock, leaving his muscles weak and his blood humming in ecstasy.

His weight on his elbows, he met her gaze, his breathing as labored as hers. She looked just as shaken by the intensity of their encounter as he was. Adam collapsed onto his side, beside his golden-eyed beauty, and snagging the first article of clothing he touched, her drawers, he swiped her belly and then his cock clean. And tossed it. The languor and tranquility pervading his body were sublime.

Quickly she turned her face away from him and swiped her cheek.

His brow furrowed, he propped himself on his elbow, slipped his fingers beneath her chin, and turned her face toward him. Tears glistened in her golden eyes.

Clearly, she noted the questioning look on his face. She smiled and said, "I'm sorry," looking embarrassed. "I'm not usually like this—emotional, that is, during or . . . after—"

"Sex?"

"Yes. I seem to keep doing this with you. Not very sophisticated of me, is it?" Her cheeks pink, she was adorably flustered. "I've never done this sort of thing—had a lover—and I've never done what we did last night ever before . . ."

Adam smiled, leaned in, and gave her a long slow kiss.

"There's no need to apologize." He knew she wasn't the sort of woman who wept easily. In fact, Marc had once stated that he'd never seen his wife cry. And he gave her plenty to cry about. Tears were something she'd obviously hidden from her husband and yet, last night and again today in Adam's arms, her social mask had fallen away. This was the third time he'd moved her to tears.

There was something about seeing them in her eyes, on her cheeks, that he found deeply touching.

"You are . . . you're a tad overwhelming . . ." Her sweet smile returned. "You're no doubt used to women who are more urbane in the boudoir."

Under no circumstances was he going to venture there. Knowing Aimee considered him no less a womanizer than Marc had been, the subject of Adam's former paramours was the very last thing he'd discuss with her. He wasn't about to make any apologies or excuses for his past.

Unlike Marc, he'd never had a wife.

"I—I suppose I should go, now that we're done . . ." She sat up.

Adam caught her around the waist before she could get any farther and pulled her back down beside him.

"We are not done, and no, you should not go. Are you forgetting the part about coming for me the rest of the afternoon and night?" he gently reminded.

Her delicate brows lifted. "I didn't think you meant it."

Adam slid his body on top of hers, his cock already stiffening against her belly. "Does it feel as though I don't mean it?" He saw a fresh flare of arousal in her eyes. *Dieu*, he loved how responsive she was. His beautiful passionate Aimee. "I haven't said anything to you that I haven't meant."

He didn't lie to women. Never made promises he didn't intend to keep. Or false declarations of affection just to entice a woman into bed.

He liked sex to be uncomplicated.

For him sex was about mutual pleasure in the moment—without the expectation of exclusivity for either party. That was how it had been with every woman he'd ever bedded.

And then there was Aimee. His fantasy come to life.

Adam kissed her again, slipping his tongue inside her mouth the moment she parted her lips. He delighted in her soft sighs and in the mounting heat sweeping through them.

Having taken the edge off his lust, he was now in better control of himself.

Just as he preferred it.

Adam rolled with her onto his back, pulling her soft form on top of him. He pressed his palm to the nape of her elegant neck and splayed his other hand on her lower back. Holding her, he luxuriated in the feel of her body against him, her taste, the warmth of her skin, letting his fingers graze along the seam of her derrière. A soft moan escaped her, and with a little wiggle, she spread her legs, allowing him to dip his fingers into the wet folds of her sex. Lightly he petted her, gently working the sensitive flesh, making her moan louder.

Though his cock was hard and desire burned in his blood, he felt as though someone had poured warm nectar over his insides. Maddeningly, lust and soft sentiment had melded. Unable to separate the two. Of the all times he'd imagined what he'd feel like after having had her, he never imagined this. Never counted on *this*.

He wanted—needed—exclusivity with Aimee. At least until this spell he was under was broken. And the novelty wore off.

CHAPTER SIX

Aimee rushed toward the gardens the next morning.

Louise was franticly looking for her.

When last they parted, it was yesterday afternoon and Aimee was on her way to search Adam's private apartments. Almost a day later, Louise hadn't seen nor heard from Aimee. She didn't blame her for being concerned, but she couldn't send any sort of message while she'd been with Adam. Upon entering her rooms not thirty minutes ago, one of her maids had notified her that Louise had spent the night waiting for Aimee in her bed-chamber. By morning, Louise had left in search of her.

Entering the Hall of Mirrors, Aimee moved along the long empty corridor and slipped out the doors leading to the vast palace gardens. Standing outside, she scanned the immediate crowd milling about and then beyond, courtiers stretching past the Petit Parc and into the Grand Parc. There was no music in the air, indicating that the King was elsewhere, his court left to amuse itself. The massive size of the gardens—manicured lawns, groves, and avenues as far as the eye could see—was going to make locating Louise a challenge, if she was here at all.

Aimee prayed Louise hadn't done anything so foolish as to venture toward Adam's apartments in search of her.

Stepping down the stone steps, she caught a glimpse of her cousin in the distance the moment the crowd to her right shifted. Relief flooded through her. Fisting her skirts, she moved briskly in Louise's direction. It was obvious she was speaking to someone, but there were too many people in between them for Aimee to tell whom.

It was only when she neared did fear slam into her chest. Louise had her head bowed, her shoulders slumped as Renault was clearly giving her a dressing-down.

Aimee all but ran the remaining distance. "Ah, there you are, Louise." She smiled and slipped a reassuring arm around her cousin's shoulders. Louise's head jerked up and surprise then relief crossed her features.

Aimee turned to Renault. The man was scowling at them. "Have you no manners, sir? Do you not offer a greeting when a lady approaches?" She got perverse joy out of reprimanding him. The man needed to be taken down a notch or two.

Renault's lips thinned. He glanced around then gave her a stiff begrudging bow. "Good day, *Madame la Comtesse*," he offered in a surly voice.

Yet again, Aimee found herself wondering what on earth Louise ever saw in this man. Any appeal he might possess was soon vanquished upon his first utterance.

"Good day, sir." Her response was curt and dismissive. "Come along, darling," Aimee said to her cousin, her arm still securely—protectively—-around Louise. She could feel the tension in her cousin's body. And her fear. She knew they were of like mind; they both wanted out of Renault's presence. The quicker the better.

"Not just yet. I asked Louise a question and she has yet to answer me," Renault interjected, arresting their steps.

Aimee let out a sharp sigh. "The answer is yes."

Renault cocked a dark brow. "Your pardon?"

"I said the answer is yes. In answer to your question: *Yes*, she does think you are a boor. Now that you are fully aware of her feelings toward you, we are leaving."

Renault stepped in front of them. "Most amusing, madame." He didn't look amused by her cut at all. She wasn't usually impertinent, but the man brought out the worst in her. "I'll need you to kindly step aside. This is a matter between your cousin and me, and none of your concern."

"I'll do no such thing. Anything concerning my cousin, concerns me," Aimee countered. "If you don't cease your harassment, I'll be forced to bring the matter to the attention of the King. He has a rather soft spot for the finer sex. He'll not take kindly to your deplorable comportment toward my cousin."

At that Renault laughed. "Madame, do you really think His Majesty would take the side of my former paramour over me, one of the most trusted men in his realm?"

Aimee narrowed her eyes and held his gaze firmly, praying he couldn't hear her heart slamming against her ribs. She hated it that he was right. Men in His Majesty's inner circle—men like Adam and Renault—had the confidence of the King. Anyone given the prestigious royal ring had the King's regard—whether they deserved it or not. Renault did not.

"Now then." Renault grasped Louise's lowered chin and jerked it up, making her gasp and Aimee stiffen. "We both know that you didn't simply accept our parting as well as you pretend. That isn't like you, Louise. You are up to something, aren't you? Why don't you tell me what it is and I may be lenient on you."

"I've nothing to say to you, Renault. Leave me alone." Louise yanked her chin from her former lover's grasp.

"Ah, now there is that temper of yours." His smile was mirthless. "The one that gets you into trouble. Again and again."

"You brought me here so I wouldn't carry on. I haven't," Louise bit back.

"No, you haven't carried on. Your behavior has been exemplary. A little too exemplary—for you. Which is why I'm suspicious. I expected at the very least badgering and begging."

It was Aimee's turn to speak up. "Clearly your conceit has made you blind to the fact that Louise has simply tired of you. My cousin does not badger or beg any man."

Renault didn't so much as glance Aimee's way. His glare remained fixed on Louise the entire time, the weight of his regard intent on intimidating her.

To Aimee's dismay, Louise lowered her gaze.

"I'm watching you, Louise," Renault said. "Whatever scheme you are hatching or already embroiled in, I can assure you that once I find out—and find out I will—I'll use the full authority of my post to see you punished for your unruly behavior. I put up with far more than I should have from you, for far too long. A *Lettre de Cachet* I think would definitely be in order. For you and"—he glanced at Aimee—"anyone aiding you."

A cold shiver raced down Aimee's spine. She felt Louise flinch. A *Lettre de Cachet* was an order signed by the King, authorizing the arrest and confinement of an individual or individuals, without trial. For an indefinite period of time. A person could be held in a prison or confined to a convent, among other places. As an abuse of their power, some men of wealth had obtained the order against ungovernable wives. Certainly if there was anyone who could obtain a *Lettre de Cachet* from His Majesty with little trouble, it was his Lieutenant General of Police.

The very man whose responsibility it was to enforce them.

"Marvelous." Aimee forced herself to smile in the vermin's face. "Should she hatch up a 'scheme' or become embroiled in one, I'm certain she'll keep that in mind. Do find someone else to annoy, Renault." She maneuvered Louise to her side and, keeping her arm around her cousin, escorted her away. Aimee kept to a leisurely pace, despite the suffocating urge to run.

"Thank you, Aimee," Louise said sotto voce. She was about to cast a worried glance at Renault when Aimee squeezed her shoulders, halting her.

"Don't you dare turn around. Keep walking. Smile. That's right. Just like that, as though you haven't a care in the world." Aimee did the same, nodding greetings and exchanging brief pleasantries with other courtiers as they made their way across the Petit Parc of the gardens of Versailles.

With her smile fixed to her face, Louise asked, "Where on earth have you been?"

"Not now. We'll act as though we are enjoying a walk. Once we reach the far end of the gardens, we'll use the avenue along the side of the palace to make our way to my apartments. We'll talk there."

*****

"I've been worried sick!" Louise exclaimed in Aimee's antechambers and began to pace, wringing her hands. "I was beside myself, Aimee! I imagined all sorts of terrible things. I thought perhaps Renault had somehow caught you in Adam's rooms. That you were under arrest."

"Well, he didn't. And I'm not."

"Yes, and I'm enormously relieved. What happened? All night I waited here for you. Did you make it into Adam's private apartments?"

"Yes."

"Did you find the ring?"

"Yes. I believe I did."

Louise let out an exuberant squeal and clapped her hands. "That's marvelous! Oh, thank heavens! Our worries are over. May I see it?"

"No. I don't have it. It's still in one of the pockets of Adam's justacorps. And before you ask, no, I don't know which one. I found it and lost it just as quickly." Aimee sighed and shook her head. "Louise, I went into Adam's rooms for your ring . . . and I came out with a lover instead."

Slowly, Louise's eyes widened and her mouth fell agape. She clamped it shut. It fell agape yet again. "A-A lover?"

"Yes. A lover. You asked me where I was all night. I was with the Marquis de Nattes. He caught me in his rooms and . . ."

"And?" Louise pressed.

Aimee walked over to the window and rested her forehead against the glass, blindly staring down at the gardens. "I gave myself to Adam de Vey . . . Repeatedly, actually."

"Re-Repeatedly?"

"Yes. Repeatedly . . . as in over and over again throughout afternoon and night." The heated image of Adam, resting on his elbows, gazing down at her, his handsome face etched with passion as he slid inside her flashed in her mind. Aimee's body warmed.

Louise burst into a fit of giggles, her joviality yanking Aimee out of her thoughts.

"What, pray tell, is amusing you?"

Louise approached, smiling, and looped arms with Aimee. "If you gave yourself 'repeatedly,' then I'd say the Marquis de Nattes's skills in the boudoir were quite good indeed."

Aimee glanced back at the gardens. "That's the crux. He wasn't good at all."

Louise's smile dissolved into a frown and she placed her hand on Aimee's shoulder. "Was it . . . terrible?"

"No." Aimee tuned around, pressed her back to the window, and leaned her head back against the glass. "It was the most incredible experience I've ever had. There is a good reason women are drawn to the Marquis de Nattes, Louise. He is far, far better than good."

"He's *that* good?"

"He is beyond compare."

True to his word, he made her come so many times, she lost count, taking her in various positions, most of which she'd never tried. All of which brought her to new heights of pleasure as the clever man found different hot spots on her body that drove up her fever. So unlike Marc, who had left soon after sex, Adam had had no interest in parting company. They'd spent hours together and he never tired of her.

Even now, away from him and his touch, his kiss, she craved him and the voluptuous sensation of his generous sex filling her so completely.

And if that weren't amazing enough, between decadent delights, he pulled her near, and lying naked with him, skin against skin, they talked. Teased. Even laughed.

Of course, she knew that being with a husband and being with a lover were different. But she also saw the glaring differences in how she responded to Adam. And how he made her feel in the aftermath.

Marc had always left her feeling sad. Inadequate.

With Adam, she simply felt wonderful.

She was still reeling from her experience with him.

"The man is altogether too perfect," Aimee said.

A squeak of joy erupted from her cousin. "I'm so delighted. You deserved to enjoy a man—especially after *Marc*," Louise said with a slight sneer. "You've got to tell me more." She grabbed Aimee's hands and pulled her down onto a nearby settee. Aimee winced when her private area came in quick contact with the upholstered furniture. Sexual excess wasn't something she was used to, but she didn't mind the twinge of tenderness. It was a reminder of her experience with Adam.

"Details!" Louise demanded. "What sorts of things did he do that made him 'beyond compare'?"

"Louise, we've got to talk about the ring."

"Yes, yes. But first answer the question. Better yet, do you think Robert is likely to be 'beyond compare,' too?"

"Louise," Aimee said firmly. "The ring. Please focus."

Louise let out a sharp breath. "I hate talking about the ring. Talking about the ring unsettles me. Especially with Renault behaving the way he is, but on the bright side, Adam de Vey is your lover. A lover who is 'beyond compare'. A definite benefit. You can access his rooms and search with ease now. Another benefit."

"It will not be with ease at all. The man is an extremely light sleeper. I tried to leave the bed, but he stirred, and well . . ."

Her cousin gave her a knowing smile. "He distracted you."

Aimee felt a blush coming on. It was embarrassing, really, for she wasn't the blushing type. Ever since she'd crossed paths with Adam at the palace, she wasn't behaving like herself at all.

"Yes, he distracted me." She admitted. "For about another hour."

And she'd loved every minute of it.

She didn't get an opportunity to search first thing in the morning either. He'd awakened her from her slumber with stirring kisses, brought her to ecstasy and back, then carried her to his *salle de bain*, where he had a warm bath prepared for both of them. Never had she shared a bath with a man.

Never had she enjoyed a bath more.

"This is all so excellent. Really," Louise stated with a grin.

"How is this excellent? We still don't have the ring and . . ." She paused.

"And?" Louise prompted yet again.

Aimee let out a sharp sigh. "And . . . it appears I am hopelessly drawn to charming roués. Like Marc. Like Adam. Men who are sure to break a woman's heart each and every time." Adam was the last sort of man she should find appealing. And yet, she found herself enormously attracted to him. If she were wise, if the ring didn't need to be found, she'd flee from the Marquis de Nattes.

But she wasn't wise. She was too captivated by Adam.

And she'd no choice but to draw near. She was going to locate that ring. In no way would she allow Louise to be at Renault's mercy.

Last night, she'd considered telling Adam about the ring, but immediately silenced the urge. He wouldn't be pleased to learn she'd lied to him, that she hadn't come to his rooms to be with him at all. It was sure to put him in a less than generous mood. And given his relationship with the King and his friendship with Renault, it was too great a risk to take.

"You don't know Adam will break your heart," Louise said.

"He will if I give it to him. And that is something I will not do."

This was merely a physical allure. Nothing more.

CHAPTER SEVEN

This was more than just a physical allure. No doubt about it.

Adam shook his head as he made his way toward his private apartments.

Merde. He couldn't believe it happened to him. He'd tried to prevent it. Stop it. Damn it, even deny it. Now there was nothing more to do but acknowledge, and accept it.

He was in love with his golden-eyed beauty.

He'd been in love with her for years.

Priding himself on his acumen, on his analytical skills, he'd completely miscalculated, downright erred in his assumption that more of Aimee would diminish his feelings and kill his craving for her.

The very opposite occurred. The more he tasted, the more he hungered. The better he knew her, the more his heart engaged.

This was foreign ground for him.

What the bloody hell was he to do now? The attraction between them was intense. That was indisputable. Mutually acknowledged.

He knew what to do there.

Courtiers were expected to be in attendance each morning as the King strolled about in the gardens, until he retired to his private apartments for his midday meal. Adam had spent day after day walking through the palace's avenues and groves with

Aimee on his arm, immersed in their own conversation, as though they were completely alone, despite the hundreds of people around them.

The inability to steal kisses had steadily driven up the undercurrent of sexual heat between them. By the time they made it to his rooms, they had at each other before the meal awaiting them. Nothing gave Adam more joy than broadening her sexual repertoire. He was amazed at just how limited her sexual experience was. Marc had been a thousand times a fool for picking his paramours over his highly responsive, stunningly sensual wife.

Adam couldn't keep his hands off Aimee. He couldn't stay away from her.

He couldn't stop thinking about her. And for the first time ever, he was having a difficult time reading a woman. Her behavior and actions ranged from downright bizarre to touchingly tender.

She was constantly surprising him.

Since arriving at the palace, there had been a series of unexpected events where Aimee was concerned.

Starting on the very first day when she'd approached him in the gardens, to the following day when he'd found her in his chambers, wanting to be taken. Having her that day had been unbalancing on several scores, not the least of which had occurred as he was driving her into a third orgasm. Shyly she'd tried to urge him to come inside her. It was a stunning request, one no woman had ever made to him before.

The thought of spending himself inside Aimee held immense appeal.

So much so, that the temptation grew stronger each time his release rushed down his cock. But he'd steadfastly refused.

He wouldn't put her at risk.

He couldn't miss the sadness in her beautiful eyes when she'd told him there would be no risk involved. That she couldn't conceive. That after three years of marriage, it was clear the problem was with her because Marc had told her about the two bastards he'd sired in his youth, prior to marrying Aimee.

There had been times Adam was angry with Marc over his cavalier treatment of his wife.

Yet at that moment, he'd never hated Marc more.

There had been no bastards.

He and Marc had been friends since childhood. Marc never withheld a single detail of his sexual exploits. He loved to brag about whom he fucked. And how.

He'd lied to his wife. Because he didn't want to admit the truth.

After bedding more women than he could count, pouring his prick into every one of them without a single offspring resulting from the unions, it was Marc who'd had the problem.

Not Aimee.

And though Adam had objected to her statement, she didn't believe him. He was left holding his tongue, unsure whether revealing the extent of her husband's infidelity would sway her or simply hurt her.

The door to his private apartments was in sight and Adam felt a smile tug at the corners of his mouth.

His meeting with the King had been preempted. A more pressing matter required His Majesty's attention.

Adam intended to change his attire.

Then look for Aimee.

With his thoughts on an afternoon of decadent diversions, and a smile on his face he couldn't vanquish if he wanted to, Adam turned the door handle and stepped into his antechamber, closing the door behind him. The sound of rapid footsteps across the carpeted floor in his bedchamber greeted him. It wasn't loud, but in the dead quiet of his chambers, it grabbed his attention.

Laurent? The older man never moved that quickly.

Adam crossed the room and stopped dead in his tracks at the threshold of his bedchamber. Stunned by the sight that greeted him.

Aimee smiled and instantly set the justacorps she had in her hands down on his bed.

The doors to one of his armoires were opened wide. A pile of clothing had been removed and was presently covering the entire surface of his bed.

"Good afternoon, Adam." Her tone was cheery.

Frowning, he took in the room, so unaccustomed to seeing his personal space in disarray. "What are you doing?" he asked, baffled.

She approached, her smile still on her face. "Oh that?" She gestured behind her. "I was waiting for your return and . . . well, I was admiring your justacorps. You know how much I adore your clothing."

He adored women, each one unique, but this compulsion she had with his justacorps was . . . odd.

Aimee's heart pounded wildly, yet she managed to maintain her smile, belying the extent of her distress.

Oh, God. She'd been caught checking his clothing.

Again.

It was bad enough having him wake up last eve in the middle of the night to find her ramming her hand into the piles, trying to repeat her actions of the day that she had successfully located the ring.

Now this.

His brow was still furrowed as he glanced at the justacorps strewn on the bed and then at her. Nervous, her smile slipped slightly. Then dissolved. "I'm sorry, Adam. I'll refold them and put them back for you." Aimee turned toward the bed, eager to appease him, cursing her bad luck.

"No. I don't think so." He walked up to her and caught her hand. "Come with me," he said and strode out of his apartments with her in tow.

Anxiety tightened her stomach. She couldn't decipher from his tone or his words if he was angry. Or worse, suspected what she was up to. *No. Impossible. How could he know?*

Because you've made so many ridiculous mistakes and have been caught too many times.

Adam led her out of the outbuildings and across the cobble-stone courtyard straight into the palace, his grip on her hand firm. Distressing.

"Where are we going?" She tried keeping her tone light, ge-nial, her pulse beating double time.

"You'll see soon enough."

Her heart plummeted when she saw they were headed to the State Rooms. Where His Majesty could be found in the after-noons attending to official business. *Heaven help her . . .*

"Perhaps you can give me a hint?" *Please!* Each day she felt more and more corrupt lying to him. Hiding the truth about the ring. Now she was simply terrified. Adam was an intelligent man. Had he indeed learned the truth on his own? Were the King and Renault waiting to see to her arrest? Had they already caught Louise?

She tried to swallow despite the knot in her throat as he marched her down the long corridor, then stopped at one of the State Room doors.

"After you," he said, then turned the door handle and swung open the door.

Taking a deep breath, she stepped inside.

Empty! Relief flooded through her. Adam gestured toward the long marble table in the middle of the room.

She drew near, noting the number of drawings covering it.

Closing the door, Adam then approached. "What do you think of my machine?"

Slowly, she walked around the table, taking in each drawing. One after another detailed a different angle of an intricate con-traption. Stopping before the final drawing, she leaned over and studied it carefully. It was the most elaborate depiction. She'd never seen anything like it.

"Is this your 'pump' machine?" she asked, glancing up at him.

A small smile graced his mouth. "It is."

Aimee dropped her gaze down to the drawings again, marveling at them. "It's incredible, Adam," she remarked from the heart, moved that he would want to share these drawings with her.

She looked up and met his gaze. *You are an incredible man.* Aimee swallowed down the words. Holding back soft sentiments, hiding the tender feelings she had for him, was becoming more and more of a challenge. She'd never had a man who shared his interests with her. Who listened so attentively to what she had to say. Or who could melt her at a glance. One look from his dark seductive eyes, one touch, one kiss, and she was lost. In sheer heaven.

Face it, Aimee, you have failed at every turn. Failed to aid Louise. And failed to guard your heart. It was as lost as the ring. And Adam de Vey had both.

His smile grew. He moved closer to her. Her heart fluttered at his proximity, his tall sculpted body now beside hers. Touching hers.

Leaning a hand against the table, he placed the other on the small of her back. "Would you like to know how it works?" he asked.

Her nerve endings were already frenzied with delight at his touch. A wonderful warmth curled in her womb. "Yes, I would love to know how it works." She meant it. She'd had many long profound conversations with him. He had a brilliant, fascinating mind.

He impressed her at every turn, with everything he did, for everything he did he excelled in. His skills in mathematics and science. His mastery in the boudoir. And Adam had accomplished something Marc never had: Adam made her feel as though she mattered.

He pointed at the depiction before her. "These large wheels right here will turn with the current of the river and work these pumps over here, scooping up great volumes of water and sending it flowing toward the reservoirs at Versailles. This machine will be significantly larger and different than the one in use at the Seine now. Part of the problem is that the reservoirs are drying up. With this machine, we'll draw more water into them, and we'll have more water to work the fountains. To that end, there will be some modifications made here at Versailles as well."

She shook her head in awe. "It's remarkable." *You're remarkable.* "Has the King approved the machine?"

Adam slipped an arm around her waist and slid her in front of him. A wave of hot arousal instantly crested over her. The bulge in his breeches pressing against her bottom was difficult to miss.

"He's considering the cost first," he murmured and grazed his mouth along her neck up to her ear. Aimee closed her eyes and luxuriated in the sensations he inspired.

She rubbed against his delicious erection, unable to stop herself, loving the soft groan she elicited from him. "Is—Is it large?"

Splaying his hand against her belly, he rolled his hips and stroked the length of his hard cock along the seam of her derrière. Drawing a moan from her. "Is what large?" There was a smile in his tone. He nipped at her earlobe.

She gasped. "The . . . co . . . cost." Oh God . . . She braced her hands against the table as he swamped her senses with another roll of his hips.

"Substantial . . . It isn't going to be easily accomplished. In fact, it's going to be quite"—he jerked his hips forward, snatching her breath—"hard." His voice had taken on that low sensual quality she'd come to know so well, her body instantly recognizing it as the usual prelude to pleasure. Her sex moistened and ached for him.

"This is the first time I've discussed my drawings sporting a stiff cock, Aimee."

Her bodice suddenly felt too tight. Too hot. She wanted to peel away her clothing, his clothing, desperate for the press of his body against hers, without any barriers in the way. "You mean you're not this excited speaking to the King?"

He chuckled softly near her ear as he opened the front of her gown. "Hardly. His Majesty doesn't distract me with his physical appeal." He slipped his hand inside her chemise, grazing it over her skin. "Are you wet for me, Aimee?" He pinched her pebbled nipple. She shuddered with a whimper.

Her breathing was sharp and quick and the sensations from his every pinch and roll of her distended nipple were melting her mind. "You know, for an intelligent man, that's rather a ridiculous question."

He released her nipple and slipped his hand out of her undergarment. Stepping away, he pushed his drawings to the end of the long marble table, then stalked up to her, picked her up off her feet, and placed her bottom down on the table. The suddenness of his actions surprised her and inflamed her further, especially when she saw 'that' look in his eyes.

The one that said, *I have to have you.*

"I don't think it's ridiculous at all. I like to hear the words from your mouth, Aimee. Are you wet for me?"

She cupped his cherished face and gave him long deep kisses, her blood rushing white-hot through her veins. He let her softly savor his mouth and she rejoiced in it, burned with it. Each stroke she gave his tongue stoking the fire. Higher and hotter. Willingly letting the flames engulf her, making the slick walls of her sex pulse with desire.

By the time he pulled away, his breathing was faster than before. "Answer me, Aimee."

"Yes . . . I'm wet for you."

"Lift up your gown. Show me."

She cast a glance at the door. They were really going to do this here? "In the State Room? What if the King—"

"The King is busy. I locked the door, and yes, here. *Now.* Lift the gown. Show me how wet you are for me." The hunger in his voice, in his eyes, was wicked and thrilling.

Grabbing handfuls of her gown, she yanked up the layers until her stocking-clad legs and caleçons were visible.

Adam pulled the ties to her drawers loose. "Spread your legs."

Holding the volume of fabrics against her belly, she spread her thighs as he requested.

"Show me," he said.

Aimee grasped the waistband of her drawers, intent on pulling off the caleçons, realizing it was going to be a bit of a struggle with her gown in her arms, if he didn't assist.

He caught her wrist, halting her actions. "Show me," he said again.

Her confusion must have shown on her face because he raised her arm and pressed a kiss to her palm, then he lowered her hand and slipped it inside her drawers, sliding her fingers down her slick folds, then slowly back up and over her clit.

She lost her breath.

Adam brought her wet fingers to his mouth. Holding her gaze, he sucked her essence off. The sweetest cream he'd ever tasted. The most potent aphrodisiac he'd ever known.

Aimee's taste.

Ravenous for more, he scooped up her legs, and placed them on the table, turning her in the process so that her side faced his front. Taking hold of her slender shoulders, he pressed her onto her back. She watched him intently as he slid her caleçons down her legs, her nervous excitement palpable. "I love the way you taste," he told her. He loved pushing her past her inhibitions. He loved the way she warmed and responded to it.

Dieu. He just plain loved her. He'd loved her forever.

He was never happier than when he was with her.

Leaning over her, he slid his hands beneath her knees, spread her thighs apart, and stopped to take in the sight of her pretty pink sex—glistening with her juices.

His mouth watered.

Starved for another taste, he lowered his head and stroked his tongue along the slit of her sex. She gave a strangled cry. Her hips shot up off the table, securing her sweet little cunt firmly against his hungry mouth.

"Adam . . ." His name slipped past her lips on a pant, her fingers digging into his arm resting across her belly.

He plied her with steady licks and sucks, making his way to that delectable bud so sensitized and engorged with excitement. Adam drew it into his mouth. Her sultry moans made his cock thicken further. Throb harder. He wanted her wetter and utterly wild.

He sank two fingers into her wet heat. Locating that sweet spot inside her vaginal walls, he stroked it with expert finesse instantly inducing the rocking of her hips and the moaning of his name.

Relishing her luscious taste, he groaned, enraptured, the sound reverberating onto her sensitive sex.

"Adam!" she called to him.

Unable to pull away, he continued to tenderly torment her clit with his lips, his tongue, his teeth, as his buried fingers worked her velvety sheath. Her feminine wall quivered and clenched around his fingers.

His cock railed inside its cramped confines, his sac tight and painfully full, and still he wouldn't pull away. This was Aimee. His Aimee. He couldn't get enough of her.

Only when she grasped his cock and squeezed it through the cloth of his tented breeches did she snag his attention away from her sex.

He jerked his head up from between her thighs and snapped it around, his lungs laboring.

"Adam . . ." She'd released her hold of him and was trying to open his breeches. "Let me taste you, too."

A request no hot-blooded man could deny.

Adam stripped off his justacorps, tossed it onto the table above her head, then opened his vest and breeches with the same impatient haste.

Freed, his cock strained out of his breeches toward her, greedy and eager.

She wrapped her slender fingers around the base of his shaft.

Brushing an errant lock from her cheek, he watched her lovely profile in heated fascination as she took him into her mouth. Wet heat engulfed him. Briefly, he closed his eyes and tightened his fingers in her hair. Her rhythm was slow and sublime.

He forced himself to hold still and not thrust despite the powerful urge, letting her dictate the depth, the pace. He was so hard. His prick was so full. And the sensations of her soft hot mouth advancing and retreating were stunning. Pre-come leaked from his cock.

She moaned with satisfaction, sending tiny vibrations racing up his prick, and then swirled her tongue around the engorged head, swiping the sensitive underside. He hissed out a breath from between clenched teeth. She had the perfect mouth. A natural talent for offering a man oral bliss. She made his sac ache. His knees weak. And because this was Aimee, his heart danced. *Jésus-Christ*, he had to decide what to do about his feelings for her. But not now.

Not when she had him completely ablaze.

Adam opened his eyes and met her gaze. His cock in her mouth as she gently worked it in and out, she was watching him intently, looking pleased with herself.

He swore. "You like arousing me to this fiery pitch, don't you, Aimee?"

She pulled him from her mouth. "I do."

"I like doing the very same to you. Would you like to come at the same time?"

"Yes!"

He smiled at her enthusiasm, despite the sexual agony he was in. "I'm going to come in your mouth," he warned, running a finger lightly over her bottom lip. "I'm not going to pull out."

"I don't want you to, pull out, that is." She squeezed his cock; a delicious jolt lanced through his sac.

Dieu, this woman was his soul mate in every way. His connection to her was so powerful—both physically and emotionally. He wanted to spend the rest of his days bringing her pleasure.

Adam leaned over her, spread her thighs wide, and lowered his mouth straight down onto his intended target, her excited clit, enjoying her sharp gasp.

She responded in kind and sucked cock into her mouth, gliding him in and out, tearing groans from his throat. Spiking his need.

The double stimulation of his cock in her mouth and his mouth on her sex was almost more pleasure than he could bear. Driving two fingers into her snug sheath, he set a rhythm she instantly responded to. He had her trembling, her juices dripping from his fingers, her little mewls sending tingles along his cock, heightening the sensations of her sucking mouth, driving him to the edge of his control.

He yanked her up tightly against him and sucked her clit harder.

She cried out against his cock, arching hard. Her rapture rocked her, her sweet cunt contracting around his fingers.

And Adam finally let go.

He came with a blinding rush into the warm cavern of her mouth. She took everything he had, spurts of come draining from his prick went on and on until he'd emptied his cock.

Adam felt her slip him from her mouth, her breathing sharp pants.

But he didn't stop, intent on milking more pleasure from her body. Kissing her silky inner thigh, he kept a concentrated pressure and measured strokes over that ultra-sensitive spot inside her sheath, overwhelming her with erotic sensations until he hurled her into a second orgasm, enjoying her wail of ecstasy, relenting only when she'd finally quieted.

He pressed a kiss to each soft thigh before he straightened up and gently eased his fingers from her.

Aimee closed her eyes, dragging breaths up her throat.

Her muscles were lax. Her body was sated and still. She didn't want to move. She wanted to pull Adam near and slip into slumber in his arms.

Forcing her eyes open, she found herself captured in his gaze. He was smiling down at her looking so beautiful. Her heart swelled with a quiet joy, the likes of which she'd never known.

He tucked in his white linen shirt and closed his breeches, then held out his hand.

Placing her hand in his, she sat up. He helped her slip on her caleçons and pulled her off the table and back onto her feet. Leaning in, he kissed her, his tongue slipping past her lips, stroking the recess of her mouth.

She sighed with deep contentment.

"When I brought you in here, I didn't intend for that to happen," he said, breaking the kiss and nuzzling her neck. "Not that I'm complaining." The smile in his tone brought a smile to her lips.

She laced her arms around him and snuggled close, pressing her heart to his. Words of how happy he made her feel, how much joy she derived from the simple act of walking through the gardens with him, talking with him, or just being by his side welled up in her throat.

She wrestled them back.

She was going to miss his kiss. Him. Terribly.

But she wasn't going to embarrass herself—or him—by declaring her affections. The last time she'd declared her affections to a man, he'd all but rejected them. Marc had certainly never returned them. This was but a sexual dalliance for Adam. Not unlike many he'd had in the past, and would have in the future.

What was remarkable for her was commonplace for him.

He'd removed his periwig upon entering the room, and Aimee threaded her fingers in his dark hair, enjoying its silky feel.

"I liked coming with you," she said softly in his ear. The only admission she'd allow herself to make.

He pressed his lips against the curve of her shoulder. "So did I."

"I want to come with you again, Adam . . . I want to come together with you inside me the next time."

He lifted his head, then pressed his forehead to hers. "Aimee, there is nothing in this world I'd love more, but I can't do that.

Marc had the problem. Not you. You're perfect. More than any man could want or hope for."

She felt a knot form in her throat. His words slipped inside her heart. No man ever spoke to her the way he did. She doubted any other man would be as convincing to her.

"Let's go to your rooms," he said, a slight smile tilting his mouth. A simple sentence, but a handful of words that held the promise of decadent pleasures. Her stomach fluttered. "We cannot go to mine. It's a tad in disarray," he gently teased her.

His innocent comment stabbed into her conscience.

She was deceiving him, voiced so many lies—when he in turn had done nothing but conduct himself with sincerity and honesty.

But how could she tell him the truth?

What could she say? What words could she offer that wouldn't diminish what they'd had? Soil the memory. He hadn't spoken of a future beyond their palace stay. She wanted him at the very least to walk away with a fond memory of their affair.

She'd cherish it always.

Someone knocked at the door, startling her. She jumped back out of his arms. Adam frowned.

Her hands flew to the front of her gown, quickly closing the fastenings with panicked haste.

"Who is it?" Adam called out, clearly irked by the interruption.

"Nattes?" Aimee recognized Robert's voice, her fingers working diligently on her gown. "I need the drawings." He tried to open the door, without success. "Why is the door locked?"

"Not now, Robert. Later."

"*Merde*, Nattes, open the door. The King wishes to proceed with the meeting. He is free now and has summoned us to his private apartments."

Adam swore under his breath. "All right. Just a moment." Turning to her, he cupped her cheek just as she finished with her bodice. "I'm sorry. I have to go."

She hid her disappointment behind her smile. "I understand. You must take your magnificent drawings to the King." She smoothed a hand over her hair then her bodice. "How do I look?"

He smiled. "Beautiful. Beautifully ravished."

She laughed. "So do you." Her comment drew a chuckle from him.

He began buttoning his vest. She scooped up his justacorps and draped it over her arm, holding it for him as his long lean fingers finished with the long row of buttons.

"Here," she said when he'd completed his task, running a quick hand down the knee-length coat to smooth out the wrinkles. Her fingers stroked over something hard and round that moved in the pocket. She froze.

The ring . . .

"Thank you." He pulled the justacorps out of her grasp and put it on.

Aimee watched helplessly as he snatched the periwig off the table, placed it back on, and strode to the door. Unlocking it, he opened it a crack. "I'll meet you there," she heard Adam say.

Robert pushed his way in. "What the bloody hell are you doing—" His words died on his tongue the moment he saw her standing near the table.

A smile appeared on his face immediately. "Madame de Gremont." He bowed.

"Please, Robert, Aimee will do just fine." She glanced at Adam's pocket and back at Robert who, still grinning, had a knowing look in his brown eyes.

"Of course, Aimee."

Her mind was awhirl as she tried to think of a way to get the ring out of Adam's pocket and deal with the delicate, rather compromising situation she found herself in. It was one thing to be seen walking about the palace gardens with the man among hundreds of courtiers, quite another to be caught alone in a locked room with him.

"I was showing Aimee the drawings for the machine," Adam offered, a frown still on his face. The look in his dark eyes gave a clear warning to Robert to choose his words carefully.

"Ah, yes, of course. And what did you think of them, Aimee?" Robert asked, being his cordial best.

"They're very impressive."

"Yes. I quite agree. It's been a pleasure assisting Adam on this project," Robert said, then to Adam, "We should gather them up and go?"

At Adam's nod, Robert collected the drawings.

Adam was about to leave. *Think!* This could end right now. End her lies to Adam. End Louise's torment. Every day that passed without the ring only raised Louise's anxieties. The strain over locating the ring was beginning to take its toll on her cousin.

Holding the drawings in his hands, Robert bowed to her. "Good day, Aimee."

"Good day." She watched Robert stride to the door.

At the threshold he tossed out, "I'll see you there, Nattes." And exited.

Adam turned to her. "I'm going to be a while. I'll see you tonight at the ball."

She smiled and nodded. "Of course." *Do something!* She rose up onto the balls of her feet and crushed her mouth to his in a kiss, and she slid her hands down his chest, moving over the brocade fabric of the justacorps, down past his waist, and lower still, fast approaching his lower pockets.

Adam caught her wrists at his hips and broke the kiss.

"Aimee, you keep that up, and I'm going to be hard," he gently admonished with a smile and placed her arms down at her sides. "I'd rather not walk into a meeting with the King with a stiff cock. Now, behave . . . until tonight." With a wink and a devilish grin on his handsome face, he turned on a heel and walked out the door.

Her heart plummeted. She was so close! She could have spared Louise another tortured night.

"Adam, wait!" He arrested his steps. She ran up to him.

His brow furrowed. "What is it, *chère?*"

Looking up at his beloved face, she wrestled with what to do. Perhaps she should tell him the truth. Perhaps it wouldn't raise his ire, after all. He was an even-tempered, reasonable man. Perhaps he'd understand about her duplicity and simply hand over the ring. And all this would be over. Dare she risk it? God knew she wanted it to be over. So badly. The ring was right there in his pocket.

"I wanted to tell you . . ." She swallowed and grappled with her words. "Well, you see . . . I . . . rather *you* . . ." Just say it!

"Aimee, the King awaits. What is it you're trying to say?"

"I'm trying to tell you that—"

"Nattes!" A male voice grabbed her attention. Her blood chilled when she saw Renault walking down the corridor toward them. Stopping beside them, the vermin met her gaze.

"Madame de Gremont," he offered stiffly.

Unlike Robert, she didn't give him permission to address her informally. Nor would she, ever. Aimee offered no more than a nod.

"Nattes," Renault said. "Where are you off to?"

"I've a meeting with the King in his chambers."

"Ah, so do I. He wants a brief word with me. I'll walk with you," Renault said with a smile and a pat on Adam's shoulder.

"Very well. Give me a moment, Sard," Adam said.

"Of course." Renault's smile faded considerably in his eyes, if not his mouth, when he turned to bid Aimee good day, then moved several feet up the hallway.

"What were you saying, Aimee?" Adam asked.

Aimee glanced over at Renault. He was leaning against the wall, the weight of his gaze squarely on her. He was too far to hear her conversation, but his presence unsettled her in the extreme.

She managed a smile. "I simply wanted to tell you how incredibly handsome you look in this justacorps." Reaching up, she smoothed the costly fabric across his broad shoulders.

His brows rose. "That's it? That is what you wanted to tell me?"

"Yes. Green is most becoming on you." *Green! Not blue or yellow. Green, Louise!* "You look exceptional in this justacorps. In fact, I believe it's my favorite of all the ones I've seen." She cringed at her prattle.

With a soft chuckle he shook his head. "You are delightfully different," he said and turned to leave.

She caught his hand. "I'd love it if you'd wear this justacorps tonight at the King's outdoor ball."

Smiling, he squeezed her hand. "I'll see." His hand slipping from her grasp, he walked away and joined Renault.

Aimee watched the two of them walk up the hallway engaged in conversation, until they turned the corner and were finally out of sight.

She stepped back into the State Room, closed the door, and slumped back against it.

Her gaze fell on the table in the middle of the room. Where Adam had given her so much pleasure.

It sank her spirits lower. She couldn't stand it any longer. She loathed the lies. He didn't deserve the deceit. He deserved the truth. Some truth. Any truth. Her heart ached just thinking about it.

Next thing she knew, she was racing up the hall toward the King's private apartments. Her heart thundered the entire way. Turning the final corner, she noted that a group of men were entering through a set of opened double doors. She spotted Adam at the back of the crowd.

"Adam!" She caught his arm the moment he was close enough to touch.

He turned around, clearly surprised by her presence. Her breathing was rapid and her heart raced, more from emotion than exertion.

"Aimee, are you all right?" His expression showed concern. "What's the matter?"

She glanced past his shoulder and saw the last man enter the King's rooms. They were alone. Fisting his justacorps, she rose to up onto the balls of her feet and gave him a soft short kiss.

He looked baffled when she released his overcoat and dropped back down onto her heels.

"I just wanted to tell you . . . I love you." There she'd said it. "That's the truth. I wanted you to know the truth." If nothing else, she was at least being honest with him, whatever his reaction.

And at the moment, that reaction was utter astonishment. He couldn't look more shocked. Uncomfortable with his silence, she began smoothing his justacorps where she'd grabbed and crinkled it. "You'd better go," she said, wanting to kick herself for the ridiculous, ineloquent way she'd just informed him of her deep affections.

"Aimee . . ." His voice was soft, but she couldn't bring herself to look him in the eye.

"Monsieur de Nattes," a tall, thin, older gentleman called to him from the doorway. "His Majesty is waiting."

"I'll speak to you later," she added with a shaky smile, turned, and walked away.

Behind her she heard the doors close. Casting a glance over her shoulder, she saw she was very much alone in the corridor.

He'd gone inside.

Excellent, Aimee. You handled that quite well. Before you had him wondering if you were mad. Now you've removed all doubt, and you've made yourself look like an unsophisticated ingénue. You certainly have a way with men.

She shook her head, her heart heavy. What a fiasco. She wanted to scream in frustration over the entire debacle. This would be so much easier if she hadn't fallen hopelessly in love with the man. And yet, despite it all, she wasn't sorry she'd told him how she felt. She only wished he'd responded in kind.

Between the lies and the love she had for Adam, this scheme was tearing her apart. The fabrications and falsehoods had to cease. This mad charade had to end. It was only getting more complicated and more convoluted by the day. One way or another, she was going to have the ring. Tonight.

She only wished she knew how.

Or what Adam was going to do next.

CHAPTER EIGHT

"Are you certain you wish to wear this one, my lord?" Laurent asked, holding up the green justacorps Adam had been wearing during the day.

Adam smiled. "Yes. That one." He knew Laurent thought it odd that he wasn't going to change into a new justacorps, as was his habit, but the golden-eyed woman of his dreams had requested to see him in it. And he was more than happy to please her.

In fact, he intended to please her the rest of their lives.

After her endearing declaration in the corridor, one that completely knocked the air from his lungs, taking him by surprise, he decided he, too, had a declaration to make.

What better place than under a starry sky with the King's finest musicians playing?

Smiling to himself, Adam slipped his arms into the sleeves. He'd chosen a different vest and black breeches to complete his attire.

"What do you think, Laurent?"

The older gentleman smiled and responded in his usual manner. "I think the lady will be most impressed, my lord."

"Ah, but this lady is very special, Laurent. She may very well become the Marquise de Nattes."

His servant's smile broadened. "She's a most fortunate woman if she does, my lord."

Adam looked at his reflection in the mirror and adjusted his sleeves. "I think I'm the lucky one."

Everything was going incredibly well. The King was most enthusiastic about Adam's machine and had given his approval to move forward on the project.

And Aimee . . . luscious, sweet Aimee was in love with him.

This night was going to be a night neither of them was ever going to forget.

"Have a good evening, my lord."

Adam couldn't seem to wipe the smile off his face. "Oh, I plan to." He turned on his heel to leave. His justacorps swung out and hit the table he passed with a *clunk*.

He stopped and glanced down, unsure what caused the odd sound. He noted that something small was bulging from his pocket.

Slipping a hand inside, his fingers touched upon a round, hard object. He pulled it out.

A ring. One of the King's rings.

Immediately, he checked his hand and found his ring securely on his finger.

This wasn't his.

Adam moved closer to the silver candelabra on the table and looked inside the ring for the inscription he knew each possessed.

R.S. were the letters inscribed. *R.S.?* One by one, he flitted in his mind through the men whom he knew had been given the prestigious royal ring.

Just then, Laurent closed the armoire's doors. The sound distracted his thoughts, yanking his gaze to his servant. Laurent moved to the second armoire and closed its doors as well. Suddenly, the image of Aimee standing in Laurent's place flashed in his head. Her hand moving over the justacorps . . . During the day. In the middle of the night. Aimee with his justacorps spread out over the bed.

Her hands moving oddly down his body—*to his pockets.*

Merde. She's been searching for this ring the whole time. R.S. Who was R . . . *Jésus-Christ*, he swore under his breath. Renault de Sard. Why was she seeking Sard's ring? Fool. Her cousin was the reason. Sard's former mistress. Sard had told him he'd ended the longtime affair while at the palace. That the woman was unbearable. Unruly. Ungovernable. And retaliatory.

He'd confided that he'd warned Louise she'd better not try anything. Had the woman taken his ring? There was no doubt in Adam's mind that Aimee was searching for it.

It became clear to Adam that she'd approached him for no other reason than to find the ring. Somehow she knew it was in one of his justacorps.

How it got into his pocket didn't matter. What mattered was that not once had he questioned her strange behavior; instead, he'd walked about in a haze of lust and love, ignoring logic. Reason. Behavior that defied explanation should have spiked his suspicions.

He curled the ring into his fist. He had one goal.

Finding Aimee de Miran.

*****

In the palace's outdoor ballroom grove, the *menuet* filled the night.

The King's musicians were situated above the cascading waterfalls, their music carrying well beyond the oval ballroom and into the surrounding woods.

A number of giant torchères illuminated the magnificent amphitheatre.

Colorful gowns and justacorps twirled past as the dancers moved in time to the music.

Sitting on one of the grass-covered steps with the other spectators, Aimee looked about. She couldn't seem to locate Louise or Adam.

Both should have been here by now. Her nerves jangled. She'd spoken to Louise. She'd told her that she was going to tell Adam everything.

Then she'd spent the next hour calming Louise down. In no way did her cousin agree with her plan initially. It took some coaxing and convincing before she ceded.

Louise was supposed to be here well before Adam. Well before now. They were going to try to explain the matter together.

A tap on the shoulder made Aimee jump and twist around. Staring back at her was Laurent.

"Madame, Monsieur le Marquis wishes to speak with you in his personal apartments."

Adam? In his chambers? "Is everything all right?"

"Please follow me, madame." The servant turned and walked away. Aimee followed, unable to shake the anxiety tightening her entrails. Dread mounted by the moment during the long walk across the gardens and to the outbuildings his master's rooms were located in.

By the time they reached Adam's door, her insides were in a frenzy.

Laurent opened the door to the antechamber and she walked in. She found Adam seated at the ebony table in the room. No justacorps or vest on, he simply wore a white linen shirt and black breeches. Reclined slightly in his chair, one arm rested casually on the table, his expression was difficult to decipher.

"Have a seat, Aimee," he said as Laurent quietly left, closing the door behind him.

Not his usual greeting. None of the warmth in his eyes or tone was there. She didn't know what to make of his mood.

Aimee sat down opposite him at the table.

He stretched out his long legs. "I've a question for you, *chère*. Actually, I have several. But we'll start with this one." He lifted his palm that was down on the table, to reveal the ring beneath it.

Aimee heart sank, knowing exactly whose ring that was.

Adam picked up the ring off the table and spun it. Silently, she watched the thing whirling on the wooden surface.

"Tell me, Aimee, have you been looking for this?"

She wasn't going to lie. Not a single falsehood would pass her lips. Whatever he asked, she was going to give him the truth. No matter the consequences, and she had a terrible feeling all was lost anyway.

"Yes. I've been looking for that."

"Why is Sard's ring in my pocket?"

"Because Louise dropped it there by accident in the Hall of Mirrors."

"And what was Louise doing with the ring in the first place?"

Aimee's gaze dropped to her lap.

"Look at me, Aimee." She lifted her gaze and met his dark eyes. "I want to hear the whole truth from you, and I want you to look me in the eye when you speak it. Understood?"

She nodded. She hated the situation she was in. She hated it that he hadn't put his arms around her this whole time. And she hated the heaviness in her heart.

"Good, now answer my question. What was Louise doing with the ring?"

"She . . . took it from Renault. She was distraught and wasn't thinking at the time. By the time she was in her right mind, she'd dropped the ring in your pocket. She begged me to help her. You know how Renault is, Adam. Or perhaps you don't know. He puts on a very different face with you than he does with Louise or me."

"So your reason for drawing near to me was the ring."

"Initially, yes, but—"

"And the day I first caught you in my room, you came not to give yourself to me but to search for the ring, is that correct?"

Dear God, that sounded so much worse coming from his mouth. "Yes, I will admit I didn't come here to give myself to you on that day, but I gave myself to you then and every day since because I wanted to."

There was a knock at the door. Adam rose, snatching the ring up off the table and taking it with him to the door. The moment he opened it, he stepped aside and muttered an oath. For the first time since she'd entered his rooms, she caught a glimpse of true ire in his eyes.

A somber man about her age stepped inside. He had two other men with him. She recognized one as being a lieutenant of Renault de Sard. She tensed.

"Monsieur le Marquis, the Lieutenant General of Police has sent us. He felt Madame de Gremont"—the man nodded toward her—"would be here. We're to escort her back to her apartments."

Aimee rose. Her stomach dropped. "Oh? Well, you may tell your superior that I am busy at the moment and whatever he wants will have to wait." Her heart pounded in her throat. Her mind spun. Her thoughts were of Louise.

Where was her cousin? What did Renault want?

Meeting Adam's gaze, she found once again he'd schooled his expression. She couldn't tell if he had something to do with the presence of these men or not.

"I'm afraid you don't have a choice, madame. It's an order," the young lieutenant said.

Fear iced through her body.

She glanced at Adam again. He said nothing. Did nothing.

He didn't believe her. Anything she'd said. No doubt including that she loved him.

How could she blame him?

Without further ado, but with shaky legs Aimee followed the three men sent for her. Afraid. And heartbroken.

*****

Standing before the door to her apartments, Aimee watched as one of the men opened it for her and asked her to step inside.

Her stomach tightened when she saw Louise in her antechamber, seated on a chair and weeping into her hands. Renault stood over her.

His usual cold glare was fixed on Aimee.

"Well, welcome, Madame de Gremont," the vermin said.

"What are you doing in my private apartments?" She managed to utter the question without her voice quavering.

"Let's not play any more games, madame. My ring is missing. And your cousin has confessed to stealing it."

Louise looked so utterly defeated, Aimee's heart went out to her. Crossing the room, Aimee sat down beside her and put an arm around her cousin. Louise immediately turned into her shoulder and wept some more.

"Your cousin says you are not involved in her thievery," Renault said. "That she acted alone. But I don't believe her."

It was Aimee's turn to glare. "She knows where the ring is. It can easily be retrieved and returned to you. There's been no harm done. You need not torment her this way!"

"I gave her proper warning of the consequences. She chose not to heed me. As usual." He threw a hateful glance at Louise. "I believe a *Lettre de Cachet* is not out of order here. Two, in fact, one for her and one for you."

That shot Louise to her feet. "Aimee did *not* steal the ring. I acted alone!"

"Yes, words from your mouth are ever so believable," Renault replied dryly. "I'll have the orders signed by the King in the morning." With that he turned and left, his men following him out. Leaving Aimee and Louise alone.

"I hate you!" Louise screamed at the closed door.

Aimee rose. "Louise, that's hardly helpful."

"I don't care. I do hate him. I can't believe I ever loved him. He isn't half the man Robert is!" Louise dropped onto the chair again, her face falling into her open palms. She cried anew. "I finally meet a decent man, one that's attentive and interested, and now I'm going to prison," Louise wailed.

Aimee moved to the door and opened it a crack. Just as she suspected. The three men were in the corridor, guarding them. She closed the door and slumped against it.

Aimee thought she, too, had finally met a decent man that was attentive and interested. Thanks to her multitude of errors and deceptions, his interest had waned. And she couldn't blame him for how he felt. She'd sufficiently earned his disdain and tainted their experience together. Sorrow surged inside her chest. She wrestled it back as best she could. Unlike Louise, she couldn't allow herself to succumb to the sadness.

Right now she needed to think of a way to untangle them from this mess.

She needed a miracle. Or three.

*****

At dawn there was a knock at the door. Louise started awake from a light sleep, while Aimee simply rose from her chair, gripped by trepidation. They had spent the night in the antechamber, too unnerved to retire to bed. Louise had drifted in and out of sleep. Exhausted, her muscles taut, Aimee had been up the entire time. It was now morning and she still hadn't come up with a viable plan to escape the trouble they were in.

Aimee cleared her throat. "Come in," she said, without glancing at Louise, knowing she'd see fear in her cousin's eyes.

The young lieutenant from the night before stepped into her antechamber, offering a bow and brief greeting to both women. "Monsieur de Saud wishes to advise you both that you are free to leave your chambers. There will be no *Lettre de Cachet* drawn up against either of you."

Louise gasped, her mouth falling agape.

Aimee was stalk still. She couldn't believe her ears. "Why the change?"

"I don't know, madame. All I can say is that the Lieutenant General of Police had a discussion with the Marquis de Nattes before changing his decision. Perhaps you should speak to him?"

Adam spoke to Renault and got him to change his mind?

A surge of hope and a spurt of joy jolted her forward. She bolted from the room and raced out of her outbuilding, across the grounds all the way to the outbuilding where Adam's apartments were located.

By the time she reached his chambers, she was flushed and out of breath. Not bothering to knock, she burst into his antechamber. Finding it empty, she rushed through his bedchamber—also vacant—to his private cabinet room. There she heard a splash. Without a moment's hesitation, she ran into the *salle de bain* and came to an abrupt halt when she found the Marquis de Nattes in his large copper tub.

Very naked.

Magnificent to behold.

She froze, her gaze sweeping over his stunning form, the sight of him inspiring an instant longing in her body and heart.

Adam fought to keep a straight face. Her expression was as amusing as it was arousing. "Good morning," he said.

"Good—Good morning . . ."

He lifted a brow. "Is there something I can do for you?"

She was softly panting, as though she'd raced all the way to his rooms. She dragged her gaze from his body up to his face, her blush turning her pink cheeks a darker hue—clearly realizing she'd been openly ogling him.

He sat up straighter, his chest rising out of the water.

"Oh, my," he heard her say softly, before she tore her gaze from his body once more and dropped it to an errant thread on her gown, plucking at it nervously. "Adam . . . I came to thank you for what you did. Whatever you said to Renault spared Louise and me an indefinite incarceration. I cannot express the depth of my gratitude."

Looking fatigued from a night of little sleep, her hair mussed, and her gown crinkled, she was still the most beautiful woman he'd ever seen. "You're welcome."

Still fidgeting with the thread, she said, "That's not all. I know you don't believe me, but I wish to say it again—from the heart—" She met his gaze. "I *never ever* once gave myself to you without desire as my motivation. It wasn't because of the ring. It was because I wanted you. I'm sorry that I lied and deceived you. I was in a difficult situation and"—she shook her head, self-disgust etched on her lovely features—"I made a mess of it all .

. . including the ridiculous way I told you I loved you. It was . . . *is* the truth, whether you wish to believe me or not. I do love you. Very much."

"I know."

Her eyes widened. "*Pardon?*"

"I said, I know. I know your affections are sincere."

"You believe me then?" she asked, incredulous.

"I believe you. When you told me you loved me in front of the King's apartments, you never tried to search my pockets as before. It was a pure utterance from the heart."

A smile lit up her face. "No, I never did! That's very true!" Tears glistened in her eyes.

"Come here, Aimee."

She approached, stopping beside the tub. Taking her hand, he pulled her down for a kiss. As she bent forward, her eager mouth met his. Adam grasped her shoulders and yanked her closer, purposely knocking her off balance and into the tub. She dropped in with a yelp and a splash.

Holding her tightly against his side, he cupped her cheek and gave her a deep, soul-quenching kiss, halting any words. Soft and languorous, he kissed her until her body yielded, and her arms encircled him, no longer caring that she was in a tub full of water, fully clothed.

He broke the kiss and grazed his lips along her jaw to her ear. "I know Marc hurt you deeply. But I am not Marc. You can trust me. I will never hurt you the way he did. I would never betray you the way he betrayed you. Your heart is safe with me. I will never treat you the way he treated you."

She pulled back to look in his eyes. Hers glistened with fresh tears. And love. And something he valued just as much—her trust. Too emotional to speak, she simply nodded, her small gesture telling him that she believed in the sincerity of his words.

And he had more to say. An admission he wanted her to hear. "There may have been women in my past, but the bulk of them have been in the last six years." He stroked her soft cheek with his knuckles. "I've spent more than half a decade looking for a woman who'll make me stop wanting you . . . I never found her. And I will no longer search. I want you and no other."

Tears of joy spilled from her golden-colored eyes. "I want no other, only you, Adam," she said. Then she kissed him. The sweetest, most heartfelt kiss he'd ever had. And he returned her kiss, until she grew hungrier, her kisses more urgent.

"I know what you need," he murmured against her mouth.

Her hand slid down his chest, moving ever lower to his stiff prick. "What is it I need?" He heard the teasing in her tone. He caught her wrist, halting her eager hand. There was one more thing he wanted to say, without those delicious distractions.

Lightly he bit her earlobe. "New clothes."

She lifted her head. Her delicate brows drew together. "New clothes?"

"A new wardrobe, only the finest fabrics, for the Marquise de Nattes."

"The Marquise de Nattes? *Me?*" she asked, so adorably incredulous.

He grinned. "Yes. You. I told Sard he wasn't going to imprison my future wife. Or her errant cousin. I pointed out that asking the King for orders of arrest for his former mistress would make him look weak. It wouldn't foster much confidence in His Majesty if his Lieutenant General of Police of Paris, a man in charge of maintaining order in a city of one hundred thousand souls, couldn't control this one woman."

She burst into laughter, and he loved the sound of it. Aimee rose up and straddled his hips. His cock jerked with delight, despite the clothing between them. "You're marvelous," she said. Cradling his face between her palms, she gave him another of her tender kisses that he felt down to the bottom of his heart.

"Since we are sharing truths," he said, opening the front of her sopping wet gown. "I love you, Aimee de Miran. I have been in love with you for so very long, I couldn't even say when it began. You're mine. This was meant to be." He brushed a wet strand off her cheek.

"I am yours," she concurred. "Today and forever. *I love you . .*." Her lips met his again, and she anxiously aided in the removal of her wet clothes, tossing each article onto the white marble floor.

"You'll stay inside me this time?" she said against his mouth.

"Wild horses couldn't stop me," he promised, slipping his hand behind her head, gently securing her soft lips more firmly to his.

Abruptly, she pulled away. "Wait, Adam. There is one more truth I want to share."

He frowned slightly. "What is it, *chérie?*"

"It's about your justacorps. They are indeed splendid, but to be quite honest . . ."

"Yes?"

"You look your best when you are wearing nothing at all."

He laughed and pulled her close. "I'll keep that in mind." Then he kissed his golden-eyed beauty with heated intensity and all the love he had for her in his heart.

EPILOGUE

In the city of Paris, there have been many weddings throughout time. But none, they say, was more beautiful or more enchanting than that of Adam de Vey, Marquis de Nattes, to his beloved Aimee.

What made this union so noteworthy was not the opulence and splendor of the nuptials, for there was definitely that. No, what brought spectators out in droves, lining the streets all the way to Notre Dame, was to see—love.

"True love" were the two words that rippled through the throng. A noble union not for political gain or advancement of power.

Just plain love.

A power unto itself.

It was said that the bride arrived wearing a magnificent golden-colored gown in a white and gold open carriage pulled by white horses. But it was her smile that people craned their necks to see. The smile of a woman in love. And she didn't disappoint the masses. Hers was as radiant as the sun.

In the spring a babe was born. A tiny boy with his father's dark hair and eyes, their little son adding to the joy in the hearts of the Marquis and Marquise de Nattes.

Some say there was magic involved in the tale of Adam and Aimee; whispers of a magical ring abounded. Others believed a miracle brought them together at the palace. While many insist it was simply written in the stars.

Destiny may have caused their paths to cross that summer.

But it was their love that made their tale romantic, repeated throughout the realm.

And ensured their happily ever after . . .

HISTORICAL TIDBIT

Louis XIV's fountain failure at Versailles was real!

And drove him crazy.

King Louis XIV had Versailles built for a number of reasons, one of which was that he hated the Louvre. He felt it was an old-fashioned palace. And the Sun King—a.k.a. the King of Bling—was nothing if not a fashionable man. :) He wanted something grand. Spectacular. New. Something befitting the most powerful monarch of the day—Louis. (Hey, after all, he ruled a kingdom of over 20 million subjects—far greater in population than England at the time). And he hired the best of the best to transform a modest hunting lodge in a country village— where Louis had played and hunted as a boy—into the Palace of Versailles.

His garden architects were to make the gardens at Versailles just as magnificent as the palace itself. And they didn't disappoint with its two hundred thousand trees, an equal amount of flowers, an outdoor ballroom (as mentioned in the final chapter in this story), a grand canal (large enough for Louis to sail small vessels), avenues, groves, cascades and multiple fountains. All of which stretched over 800 hectares of land.

And Louis thoroughly enjoyed his massive gardens. (He hated the indoors and believed indoor air was unhealthy).

But the amount of water needed to supply the palace fountains exceeded what was available, even with the rerouting of several rivers in the area and exhausting other neighboring water supplies. Unfortunately, Louis's fountains couldn't spray at the same time. And so, they would be turned on one at a time as Louis strolled by and turned off once he left that particular area of the gardens. This water deficiency was unacceptable to the King.

He wanted a solution. And he asked Royal Academy of Sciences, formed in 1666—(an engineering body that the hero of this story belonged to)—to solve the water problem at his palace. After entertaining a number of different plans and suggestions, the Marly Machine was created—a marvel of the seventeenth century. An engineering feat, really. Built on the Seine, it was a large hydraulic system with two hundred and fifty pumps that pumped vast amounts of water from the river Seine all the way to Versailles. Did it work? Well, it had its hiccups. And some breakdowns. Some of the underground pipes burst. And it was enormously costly to build (about one hundred million in today's dollars)—with addition costs to maintain. (Maybe if Adam had worked on it, it would have functioned better. *winks*) In the end, Louis XIV never had his fountains working at full pressure—as they do today. Monies were eventually diverted for war, and expanding the kingdom.

As to the Lieutenant General of Police, that too was real! It's true! The character of Renault de Sard is based entirely on the first Lieutenant General of Police of Paris, Nicolas de la Reynie. The office was inaugurated in 1667. Long before London's Bow Street Runners (formed in 1749), seventeenth century Paris had a police force whose job it was to protect the public. Good thing. Murders happened in Paris daily. Reynie's advanced views of law enforcement helped establish the foundation of modern policing. (Watch for Renault de Sard in an upcoming Fiery Tale, THE PRINCESS & THE DIAMONDS. He has an important mission for the hero of that Princess & the Pea inspired tale.).

The glittering court of Louis XIV wasn't just salacious and elegant. It was the very time period that the father of fairy tales, Charles Perrault—author of *The Tales of Mother Goose*—wrote stories that have delighted generations: *Sleeping Beauty, Little Red Riding Hood, Puss in Boots, Bluebeard* and the ever popular, *Cinderella,* to name a few.

I hope you enjoyed your time in the opulent world when fairy tales were born. Please see the end for a delicious excerpt of yet another Fiery Tale!

Happy reading!

GLOSSARY

Antechamber　　The sitting room in a lord's or lady's private apartments (chambers) within their hôtel or château.

Caleçons　　Drawers/underwear.

Chambers　　Another word for private apartments. A lord's or lady's chambers consisted of a bedroom, a sitting room, a bathroom, and a *cabinet* (office). Some chambers were bigger and more elaborate than others. Some *cabinets* were so large, they were used for private meetings.

Chère　　Dear one. (French endearment for a woman, *cher* for a man).

Chérie　　Darling or cherished one. (French endearment for a woman, *chéri* for a man).

Comte/Comtesse　　Count/Countess.

Dieu　　God.

Duc/Duchesse　　Duke/Duchess.

Hôtel/Château　　The upper class and the wealthy bourgeois (middle class) often had a city

	mansion in Paris (*hôtel*) in addition to their palatial country estate(s) (*château*).
Justacorps	A fitted knee-length coat, worn over a man's vest and breeches.
Lettre de Cachet	Orders/letters of confinement—without trial—signed by the King with the royal seal (*cachet*).
Merde	Shit.
Ma belle	My beauty. (French endearment for a woman).
Salle	*Room.*
Salle de Bain	*Bathroom.* A small room located in one's private apartments/chambers in either a château or hôtel. The room usually had a fireplace, a tub, and a toilet (that looked like a chair with a chamber pot). The room was small on purpose so that the fire from the fireplace would keep the space warm while one bathed.
Salle de Buffet	*Dining Room.*

READ AN EXCERPT OF
THE LOVELY DUCKLING

Inspired by the tale of The Ugly Duckling, an erotically charged historical romance novella from the acclaimed Fiery Tales series.

Reputed for his carnal skills, notorious rake, Joseph d'Alumbert, prefers amorous encounters without any sort of emotional entanglement—until a quick-witted, most unique lady stirs tender feelings and hot desire.

Emilie de Sarron suffered burns to her body as an infant, and keeps her scars—and her heart—well hidden. But Joseph is determined to peel away her inhibitions, one slow steamy kiss at a time, to reveal the beautiful swan inside...

***Originally published in THE PRINCESS IN HIS BED anthology.

*An "ugly duckling" is someone who blossoms
beautifully after an unpromising beginning.*
*—Eric Donald Hirsch et al., The New Dictionary
of Cultural Literacy, 2002*

CHAPTER ONE

"*Details*, Vincent. You cannot simply state you had two women last night without offering *details*," Gilbert complained, sporting his usual lazy smile.

Joseph d'Alumbert, rose from his plush chair and strode across the floral carpet over to the window in the antechamber—away from his twin brother Vincent and younger brother Gilbert. He knew full well Vincent wasn't about to withhold a single salacious detail of his evening of excess.

He simply wanted their younger brother to beg a little.

"Ah, the details . . ." Without turning around, Joseph knew his twin was grinning. He heard it in his tone. Though he and his brothers ordinarily shared the particulars of their carnal encounters, at the moment, Joseph didn't care a whit how Vincent's evening had unfolded.

He was on edge. Worse, since his arrival yesterday at the Comtesse de Saint-Arnaud's country estate, he found himself looking out the window at the courtyard one too many times.

And here he was. Doing it *again*.

Joseph braced his hands on the window frame as he gazed down at the empty cobblestone courtyard. It was late afternoon. The Comtesse's week-long masqueraded affair was into its second day. Well under way. *She's not coming*, he mentally willed.

"*Well?*" Gilbert prompted Vincent, impatience in his tone.

"He had the d'Esseur sisters, Gilbert," Joseph responded for his twin. "There's nothing new there. Everyone has fucked them."

"I haven't!" Gilbert said. "How were they, Vincent? How can you be certain it was them? Everyone's identity is disguised."

Vincent chuckled. "Dear brother, you have been away in the campaign too long. Marie and Jeanne d'Esseur are known for two things. Their talented mouths. And their unfortunate, distinctive laugh . . ."

The Comtesse's parties were never short on decadent diversions—to suit just about any taste. Yet last eve, instead of indulging in some debauchery of his own, Joseph had spent it in the company of the Comtesse's fine brandy. Unable to focus on the amusements at hand, he'd actually turned down women who were eager to engage in just the sort of impersonal copulation he preferred.

His thoughts were being pulled toward a female who wasn't even in attendance.

"Fine. Wonderful. They had a distinctive laugh," Gilbert said. "What else, Vincent? Out with it. Tell me before I stop asking altogether."

At that, Vincent laughed. "We both know you won't," he needled Gilbert. "But since you *insist*, I shall tell you . . . I had them in the gardens, behind the statue of Zeus . . ."

A black carriage pulled into the courtyard, capturing Joseph's attention. His brothers' voices immediately faded into the distance as he watched it halt before the main doors of the Comtesse's château. Sunshine glinted off its top.

He tensed.

Moments later, a figure alighted with the aid of the footman. She wore a mask. And a wig. But it didn't matter. It was *her*. He'd know her anywhere. The way she was dressed—the multiple layers of fabrics—made him certain.

Merde.

He'd hoped he'd convinced her to stay away. He knew exactly what she was after. Her letter had stated it plainly. She was here for the same reason everyone attended the Comtesse's gatherings.

For the carnal entertainment.

For anonymous sex.

Joseph tightened his jaw and held back the expletives thundering in his head. He wasn't about to let his brothers know how discomposed this woman had him. He'd never live it down. Women didn't normally stir him beyond the physical. Yet lately Emilie de Sarron had been affecting him on a number of disquieting levels.

Jésus-Christ, she didn't belong here. Not with this group. At hand were the very people who had driven her into seclusion ten years ago.

He was among the guilty.

He'd been a party to her humiliation the night Emilie had been introduced into society. As son of the Duc de Vernant, it wasn't his habit to take stock of his behavior back then. He did as he pleased. Behaved as he willed, without thought or concern. Without excuses or apologies. But the hurt he'd seen in her soft green eyes before she turned and left was still vivid in his mind. Still ate at his conscience. Even after a decade.

She'd withdrawn from society after that night.

She was never betrothed. Never married. He'd never seen her again until last year when he spotted her at the theater. And she looked beautiful; her pale-colored hair and light-colored eyes had always been a stunning combination. Yet the many layers of clothing she wore were a sobering reminder of what made Emilie different from everyone else.

Driven by a need to know how she'd fared all these years, Joseph had sent her a letter the next day. He never imagined she'd be so delightfully witty. Refreshingly frank. Surprisingly bold.

A year later he was still corresponding with her.

The more he got to know the real Emilie, the more he liked her. And the worse he felt for the impact he'd had on her life. A life that might have turned out very different had the incident ten years ago not occurred.

But he couldn't change the past no matter how much he wished it.

Emilie was the only one to affect his conscience when his conscience had never bothered him before. She was the only one to inspire a troubling sense of possessiveness. Or a level of interest he didn't normally offer women.

Limiting the women in his life to bed sport, the rapport he had with this particular female was novel. He'd never touched her, never tasted her, yet he knew her more intimately than any woman he'd ever bedded. Emilie was restless, looking for a reprieve from her staid existence. She longed for a bit of gaiety. She was starved for a taste of passion.

And she was intent on using the anonymity the masquerade offered to disguise her identity, in order to sample some.

Just imagine the stir it would cause if the Comtesse's guests were to learn Emilie de Sarron was back. After ten years of self-imposed exile.

"Are you listening to anything I'm saying?" Vincent's voice cut through his thoughts. Joseph reluctantly pulled his attention away from the window.

His twin approached, stopped beside him, and looked down at the courtyard. "Well, well. A new lady has arrived. Do you know who she is?"

"No," Joseph lied.

Gilbert moved to the window and studied Emilie as she spoke to the footman. "What difference does it make who she is?" He grinned. "Someone new to play with."

An objection shot up Joseph's throat. He swallowed it back down.

He'd no right to object. Emilie was free to have sex with whomever she chose. This was something she wanted, and he wasn't going to interfere in any way. He'd offered his concerns about her intentions. Clearly, she'd chosen to proceed nonetheless. He had no idea how badly she'd been burned as an infant, but that fire had changed her life forever, scarring her body permanently. Scars she kept hidden beneath her clothing.

Just how easily a man would detect them during sex, he'd no clue. Her injuries were one of the few topics they had never touched upon in their letters.

The one thing he knew for certain was that *he* wasn't going to be the one deflowering her. No matter how stirring her latest letters—filled with sexual curiosity and sensual yearnings—had been.

He'd done enough to her already.

If she felt confident she could indulge in an amorous encounter without anyone identifying her or discovering her scars, then that should put an end to his disquiet.

But it didn't.

The idea of her giving herself to one or more of the men in attendance actually plagued him, and he had no idea why it should.

If that weren't bad enough, he had another problem. A sizable one.

Emilie had given him her trust, something he knew she didn't offer just anyone. And he was lying to her.

Knowing she wouldn't correspond with him if he'd used his name, he'd misled her in his first letter. And in every letter since. Emilie de Sarron believed that the man she'd opened herself to, confided her most intimate thoughts and longings to—was his brother Vincent.

Joseph was too far into this now. To reveal his deception would only hurt her terribly and that was something he couldn't bring himself to do to her. Not again.

Somehow, some way he had to get through the rest of the masquerade without Emilie—or Vincent—discovering his lie.

Just how the bloody hell was he going to maintain the ruse *here?*

Emilie stepped around the footman and walked into the château. Joseph turned on his heel and snatched up his mask.

"There is a party under way. I'm off." He marched out of the room without a look back.

Gilbert turned to Vincent. "Well? Shouldn't we join in?"

Vincent glanced down at the courtyard, noting the woman was gone. He smiled good-naturedly. "Absolutely. I believe the first thing I'm going to do is acquaint myself with the newly arrived lady."

*****

"You're here!" Beaming, Pauline de Naylon, Comtesse de Saint-Arnaud, stepped around the desk in her library toward Emilie, her arms wide open.

Removing her demi-mask, Emilie smiled at her aunt, hoping she didn't look as nervous as she felt. Her heart had pounded the entire trip from her town house in the city to the Comtesse's country estate. The closer she got to the Comtesse's château, the more she wrestled with her courage. What she was doing was daring. Risky. A tad foolhardy. She'd purposely distanced herself from many of the guests and their vicious tongue-wagging years ago.

It took everything she had not to turn and run back into hiding.

Pauline embraced her warmly and pressed her cheek to hers. "I'm delighted you came."

"Hrrmph." Twenty years Emilie's senior, her cousin Marthe d'Arbac, Marquise de Sere, scowled from the doorway. She'd all but dragged her feet from the Comtesse's main doors to the library. "Your invitation has drawn her into the Den of Iniquity. What is there to be delighted about?"

"Ah, Marthe." Pauline's smile faded. Her tone was flat. "You made the trip, too. It was lovely of you to accompany Emilie. Feel free to take your leave at any time." Pauline looped arms with Emilie. "She's in good hands now."

Marthe lifted her chin a notch and clasped her hands before her. Emilie sensed it was likely to keep herself from strangling

Pauline. The two women had maintained an unwavering animosity, stemming from their court battle where Marthe and her husband, the late Marquis de Sere, had won guardianship of Emilie as a child and control over her vast fortune until she came of age—years ago. Pauline from her mother's side and Marthe from her father's side of the family, the only things they had in common were their age. Their widowhood. And their affection for Emilie.

Marthe's eyes narrowed. "I'll not abandon Emilie in this . . . *place*. It's utterly shocking what you allow in your home. Public fornication."

Emilie sighed. "Marthe, that will be quite en—"

"I allow private fornication as well," Pauline said. "Perhaps if you had a man more often, Marthe, you wouldn't be quite so shocked."

Emilie mentally cringed. A battle was afoot.

Just as expected, Marthe fired back. "Oh, you . . . ! You are utterly *brazen!* You see what I mean, Emilie? She is shameless. She always has been. We should get back in the carriage and return home immediately."

"She has been cloistered long enough!" Pauline countered, releasing Emilie's arm. She pointed an accusatory finger at Marthe. "You're to blame. You and that horrible late husband of yours—"

Emilie took a deep breath, striving for patience. The last thing she needed was bickering between her kin. Her nerves were far too frayed. She'd come looking for a break from the monotony in her life. But this wasn't the sort of entertainment she had in mind.

Both women meant the world to her.

If she hadn't wanted Marthe and Pauline to repair their rift, she'd have left Marthe behind, given her own carnal intent. Perhaps it was too ambitious to plan on enjoying a lover *and* bringing Marthe and Pauline together after all this time, hoping they'd finally make peace.

Emilie held up a hand to silence them and implored, "Enough. Both of you. *Please*. Darling Aunt Pauline, you simply must attempt to be nice to Marthe."

Pauline crossed her arms. "She doesn't make it easy. She's entirely too single-minded and obstinate."

Marthe sucked in a sharp breath, indignant. Emilie walked over and placed an arm around her. Giving her an affectionate squeeze, she quickly stemmed Marthe's flow of hot words. "Qualities you both share at times, no?" she asked, looking pointedly at both women.

Marthe clamped her mouth shut and looked away. Pauline simply studied the state of the nails on her left hand. Both refused to admit the truth.

Taking advantage of the silence, Emilie continued. "Now then, we've discussed this," she said to Marthe. "I'll not be dissuaded. I'm seeing this through. If you don't wish to stay, you may leave. I shall see you at home in a week."

"But Emilie . . ." Marthe said. "What you're planning to do . . . You're actually contemplating your own *ruin*. You don't belong here. You are not like these women."

Those words had bite, though Emilie knew they were innocently dealt.

She smoothed a hand down her cloak. It was summer. A cloak wasn't needed, but she wore one anyway. She owned several, various colors, various fabrics. Heavy to light. Ornate to plain. For every season. The more she covered her body, the more confidence she had. It was something she'd done since she was a child. It hadn't stopped the ridicule. Nothing ever had.

It gave her a certain comfort to envelope herself within the coverings of fabric. A barrier between her and the outside world.

But she was tired of the way she lived.

Tired of living vicariously through the characters in the books she read, the theater she frequented on occasion, and the precious few friends she corresponded with.

Tired of not really living at all.

Her discontent had become so deep, it had dragged her out of her safe solitary existence straight into one of the Comtesse's notorious masquerades. "You are correct. I am not like these women. Or any woman. Thanks to the scars," she said. "And no amorous encounter could bring about my ruin. My ruin happened long ago in a fire that took the lives of my parents and left me in this rather sorry—unmarriageable—state."

Marthe lowered her head, clearly remorseful of her words.

"Love and marriage are beyond my reach. I've made my peace with that," Emilie said. "But I refuse to live out my life without ever knowing a taste of passion."

As long as it was real and as scintillating as the passion she'd read about.

"If passion is what you want, then that is exactly what you shall have, *ma chère*," Pauline said. "Besides, marriage is highly overrated. Trust me, I should know. I was married to the Comte de Saint-Arnaud. A lover is much more preferable than a husband. You can easily change a lover."

Marthe's head shot up. "Have you no decency?"

"Oh, hush, Marthe." Pauline walked up to Emilie and pulled her away from her older cousin. "You are going to enjoy yourself this week."

"But—But—what if they recognize her?" Marthe asked. "You know what they did years ago—"

"No one will recognize me," Emilie cut her off abruptly, not wanting to remember that night. Or talk about it. She knew Marthe meant well. Unlike her husband, the Marquis de Sere, who had been more interested in Emilie's inheritance than in her, Marthe's concern for her was genuine. "After such a lengthy absence, no one will think for a moment that I'd be in attendance. Besides, everyone wears masks at all times and even costumes. Isn't that so?" she asked Pauline. Her layered mode of dress wouldn't look odd here.

"Yes. The ladies especially. They make every effort to maintain their anonymity—with both elaborate masks and outfits. I find men don't make as much of an effort to conceal their identities, but they, too, wear the required mask. And no one, absolutely no one, is permitted to unmask anyone here. However, if during a carnal encounter, in a *private* setting, one chooses to reveal oneself, then that is between the lovers at play."

Marthe slapped her hands over her ears. "I can't listen to this."

Pauline's smile broadened at Marthe's discomfort. "There are plenty of men here to choose from, Emilie. Many of them were not there that horrible night."

Pauline's response made Emilie's heart flutter. There was a very special man somewhere in the Comtesse's home, one who wasn't part of that incident a decade ago.

Vincent d'Alumbert.

He'd mentioned in his letter that he, too, would be in attendance at the masquerade. She'd only ever seen him once, from afar, a long, long time ago. She was so eager to see him up close and in person. More than she could ever admit. Probably more than she should.

But she couldn't help having tender feelings for him. He and his letters were a source of joy. She felt so very close to him, having forged a connection with him she'd never had with anyone else. There was nothing she couldn't ask him. Or tell him. And she'd divulged plenty.

Given what she was attempting to do—indulge in debauchery—it settled her nerves just knowing he'd be present. On hand to offer advice if she needed it.

Pauline donned her silver-colored demi-mask with white plumes, then approached, placed her hands on Emilie's shoulders, and looked her firmly in the eye. "Are you absolutely certain you want to do this?" she asked.

Emilie tamped down her fears and self-doubt and steeled her courage. "Yes." Just once she wanted to be desired. For the next few days, she was going to step into the world of make-believe. With the aid of her masks, be transformed into someone else. For the first time ever, she wasn't going to be looked at as a misfit. Or damaged. She wouldn't be *Emilie Embers. Singed Emilie de Sarron.* Or equally as detestable, *The Ugly Little Duckling*—cruel names she'd endured all her life.

She deserved to be wanted. Kissed. Touched. Held. Every woman did, no matter her plight.

"Very well. Then let us begin." Pauline took Emilie's demi-mask of gold and red from her hand and tied it in place. "There's no time like the present." Looping her arm with Emilie's once again, she led her to the door. "You don't have to worry about approaching the men. They'll no doubt approach you."

THANK YOU for reading THE MARQUIS'S NEW CLOTHES!

Want my next release for just **99¢?** Sign up for my **99¢ New Release Alert** newsletter at www.LilaDiPasqua.com. Each new release will be **99¢** for a SHORT time only. Get notified. Don't miss out!

FIERY TALES SERIES

Novellas
Sleeping Beau
Little Red Writing
Bewitching in Boots
The Marquis's New Clothes
The Lovely Duckling
The Princess and the Diamonds

Holiday Novella
The Duke's Match Girl

Anthologies
Awakened by a Kiss
The Princess in His Bed

Full-length novels
A Midnight Dance
Undone
Three Reckless Wishes

Lila DiPasqua is a *USA TODAY* bestselling author of historical romance with heat. She lives with her husband, three children and two rescued dogs and is a firm believer in the happily-ever-after. You can find her on Facebook, Twitter, Instagram, and Goodreads!